Aleister through the Looking Glass

Robert G. Makin

Second printed edition ISBN: 978-0-9887553-8-3

Layout, interior design and cover design by Jonni Anderson:
      jonnianderson.com, starwatchcreations.com

Cover photo copyright © 2009 by Robert G. Makin

Sons of Aaron Publishing

Palm Coast, Florida

Acknowledgments

Poking fun at frustration is never more fun than when the frustration belongs to everyone else who tries to do the same thing and fails for the same reasons. Seeing the humor, though, often eludes us. It's only in hindsight that, after overcoming obstacles, one can laugh at and parody the struggle.

A few years ago, in an email conversation with Jack D. Hunter, he relayed to me the same feelings of frustration with the publishing infrastructure that I was feeling and for the same reasons. As a many-times-over #1 Best Selling author, Jack, at the same time, surprised me and uplifted me. He told me he found a solution to the problems he was facing and in that solution, I found hope and direction. I chose to take the same path he said he did. I wish he were still alive so I could thank him personally.

Such encouragement shapes our lives. I had many teachers, friends and family who when I was hungry for encouragement, fed me. To list them would be impossible, but I'd like to mention one, another who has traveled into "that undiscovered country from whose bourne, no traveler returns." Ray W. Knapp, a professional enabler of those who would try to write in English, was undiscoverable when I tried to find him to send him a copy of *Return To Masada*, my first book. Ray had passed away several years before. These are some of the people, who when I thought I was a Mole or a Cricket, reminded me and helped me to come to believe that I am actually *ME*.

As Clint Eastwood said in *Dirty Harry*, "a man's got to know his limitations." So, for manipulating artwork, graphics and certain editing services, I rely on Jonni Anderson's help. She consistently finds things I overlooked, regardless of how carefully I review before sending her my stuff. If my books present an appealing presentation, it's thanks to her. All I did was put in the words.

I suppose the most important inspirations for *Aleister through the Looking Glass* are the literary agents and publishers who provided grist for my mill through real life experiences. *Aleister through the Looking Glass* may sound like fiction, but I swear, every word is true, on some level.

Forward and Dedication

I met a little boy, many years ago (1974), Andrew. He was about eight years old. One day, in school, his teacher asked him, "Who are you?" Many of his fellow classmates already answered the question with their names, their lineages, their hobbies. When Andrew faced the question, he thumped his chest with his thumb and answered, "I am ME!" I did not witness this. His teacher related this, saying, "He followed the answer with a big grin." That was so "Andrew."

No human being faced with that question could make a statement more true or profound than that!

We human beings, by nature, feel uncertainty, self-doubt and inadequacies. We live in them. They shape our lives, our hopes and our loves. We bolster ourselves in the face of those things by falling into and relying on "Belief Systems," that comfortably define us. Part of the "Belief System" of fledgling writers is the absolute faith that those with more experience, who give us advice are 'right on' in their evaluations of US and our work. The caricature of the Literary Agent who can turn people into other animals is not allegory or exaggeration. It's real. When Ronald Flaass turned Crystal Gooseberry into a Goose by simply saying "You're just a Goose," her faith in his judgment made it a fact — for her, as a function of the respect she held for his alleged judgment and knowledge.

The fledgling writer, Aleister, learns the power and necessity of self confidence, self determination and above all to not place his faith in the words of those who hold themselves out to be devas and demi-gods. One's own decisions are the final factors in determining what and who one is. It takes great self confidence, which Andrew certainly had, to hold one's self out in defiance of the categorical definitions set by others and announce to the world, "I am ME!"

**This book is dedicated to
Andrew Parker Allis**

I hope he is still as strong and free of spirit
as when he was eight years old.

Contents

Aleister through the Looking Glass

Robert G. Makin

Chapter 1: The Trap

BANG! The explosion destroyed Aleister MacCorkadill Smiley's dream. It blasted him out of a date with a brown eyed, super model named H'eung Yau. The ear shattering explosion interrupted their first kiss. He awoke in a rage, realizing crushing disappointment that H'eung Yau existed only in his dreams and the explosion ripped her from him right there in his bedroom.

Well, it could be called his bedroom. The sparsely furnished, fifteenth floor, walk-up had one room and something in it just blew up. Aleister's anxiety skyrocketed as little pieces of paper fluttered to the floor, some of them still smoking.

He tried to leap out of his bed, but discovered the mattress resting on top of him. Dragging himself out from under it, he saw his table for two, which he used for a desk, upside down and halfway across the room, its two chairs sprawled on their backs on the floor. Papers and books from the table littered the room.

Loud pounding on the wall interrupted his turmoil. "What's goin' on over there? Be quiet! People are tryin' to sleep! Sounds like a war!"

Frantic, Aleister thought first of his manuscript. He had left it on the table, but now it littered the floor. His lap top computer in its case in the corner, remained where he left it. He could see it in the light from the billboard across the street. *Well, the saved copy should be okay.* He felt for the thumb disc on the lanyard around his neck. It was still there. If the explosion damaged the hard copy, he could always print another one, that is, when he got the money to buy paper again — and ink.

His bedside lamp rested on its side with a broken shade. He felt his way across the room looking for the wall light switch, when he noticed a strange light flashing from under one of the books, swept off the table in the explosion. Aleister stumbled over a shoe lying on the floor. He found the light switch and flicked it on. The distinct sound of chuckling caught his attention. Glancing around the room, his eyes locked on his bedside stand.

Unbelievable!

He tried to remember if he'd been drinking the night before, then it laughed once loudly and the winged monkey vanished in a puff of green light. *Impossible. I'm not awake yet. This is not the Land of Oz. I'll forget I saw that. Yes. I already forgot it. Now. What's that flashing?*

It came from under a book on the floor, *The Writers' Market*, partly concealing the newspaper. *What could that be?* Last night, he had left it on the table opened to the Classified Page, after spending hours searching for a job. He left the newspaper on the table, with his latest manuscript. One of the want ads still flashed. He lifted the table off the floor and restored it to its upright position, looking around cautiously, trying to figure out what caused the explosion. Restoring one of the chairs to its original position, Aleister sat down to read the green, flashing ad.

> *Prestigious Literary Agent Seeks Office Assistant.*
> *Quiet working conditions. Good benefits.*
> *Apply in person to:*
> *Ronald M. Flaass and Associates*
> *152732⅔ Fifth Floor, Pith Avenue*
> *New York, New York*
> *Pay commensurate with experience.*

He had never before noticed a flashing advertisement in a newspaper and couldn't understand how he missed it last night. *I wonder if the winged monkey had anything to do with this. NO! I've already forgotten that. Winged monkeys don't exist.* Aleister tried convincing himself that he saw the monkey because of the explosion, but that couldn't have happened, either. *Maybe it was part of the dream?* There was nothing there that could explode. His eyes returned to the newspaper. *And this flashing ad from Flaass is some kind of advertising gimmick.*

Aleister arrived at 8:00 A.M., just in time to hear the click as the door unlocked itself. The heavy, wood frame door displayed a big office sign on a translucent glass window, stating simply

"Ronald M. Flaass, Literary Agent."

He opened the door and walked in, finding himself alone. In the center of the room stood a large, ornate desk and chair. In the center of the desk rested a rubber stamp and inkpad. Neatly arrayed packaging material, string and packing tape gave the desk the appearance of crude efficiency. In one corner of the room, an antique, standing floor mirror and small end table disrupted the continuity of the office.

Aleister hated mirrors and didn't even own one. He knew what he looked like and didn't need to be constantly reminded of it. At 5'7" his very short blond hair topped off a long, thin nose, weak chin and fierce, blue eyes. The scar under his right eye reminded him of a bully with a big ring on his finger, in grade school, who used to take pleasure in hurting him. Wearing latex gloves most of the time when away from his apartment protected him from having to touch things that might have germs on them. He weighed one hundred ten pounds and every time he thought of that he remembered his mother's comment when he was a boy. "If he lives, he'll put on weight when he gets older." But nothing changed. At thirty-two years of age, he still weighed one hundred ten pounds.

Stacks of packages littered the room. All addressed to Ronald Flaass, Literary Agent. He noticed a note between some stacks of paper on the desk. The first stack said, "Instructions to all applicants. Fill out the application form in Stacks two and three. Sign it. Leave it on the table next to the floor mirror. Come back tomorrow. If your name's on the desk, you got the job. Instructions for fulfilling the job requirements will be supplied at that time."

As he began filling out the application forms, something caught his eye in the direction of the mirror. He glanced up. He noticed nothing amiss, but when he looked up, he saw an unusual painting hanging on the wall beside the mirror. It portrayed a hauntingly beautiful young woman who oddly resembled his dream, super model, H'eung Yau. This lady, though, wore a pointed hat, like a witch's hat, made of a black shiny material that gleamed in whatever light the artist used.

The winged monkey sitting on the woman's shoulder riveted Aleister's eyes to the painting and he thought both of them were watching him. Their eyes followed him, as he walked across the room toward the painting, for a better look. In addition to the hat, she wore a textured cape of some sort, over a dark blue gown. *Made up for Halloween, I guess. Or maybe, it's from the front cover of one of the books Flaass handled.* At that thought, Aleister had the distinct impression that the lady in the painting smiled a little more broadly. He felt fairly certain, he heard a chuckling sound much like the monkey in his apartment the night before.

He immediately stopped looking at the painting and returned to the desk to complete his job application. *There are no winged monkeys,* his thoughts insisted. As he pulled the chair out from under the desk to sit down, its legs screeched against the wooden floorboards. In contrast to the silence of the place, the sound jarred his nerves. *This place is just too weird, but a job's a job and a man has to do what he has to do to survive.*

Other, equally strange paintings decorated the walls. One depicted an enormous lady standing before a podium with a microphone in her hand, singing. Tiny, but very rotund people gathered all around her to listen. Aleister quickly looked away from that one, too, because he had the distinct impression that when he looked at her, she winked. Another painting displayed a crowd of people gathered around a piano. They stretched their arms over each other's shoulders like old friends. Some held beer glasses and one held his glass to his lips as though about to take a sip. They sang some tuneless song accompanied by the pianist but Aleister couldn't hear the song or see their faces. Cardboard boxes worn on all their heads concealed them from view.

Aleister tried to not pay any more attention to the strange paintings. The door opening from the hallway broke his attention. A heavyset, middle aged man came in pulling a dolly behind him, loaded with more packages. The man wore a deliveryman's uniform labeled FEDUPS Delivery Service. "Well, glad to see they finally got someone working here. Where do you want them, sonny?" he asked jovially, as he began unloading the dolly beside the mirror.

"But I don't work here, uh, yet. I'm just filling out the application." The uncertainty in Aleister's voice was obvious even to Aleister.

"Oh you'll get the job," the FEDUPS man assured him, glancing at the stacks of packages all around the room. "They really need the help. And I hear they pay well, too, so you'll probably accept the job if they offer it."

"What happened to the last guy?" asked Aleister. "I mean, uh, do you know what happened to him?"

FEDUPS let go of the dolly and scratched his chin thoughtfully. The dolly went to an upright position and waited for him. "I really don't know," the man answered. "He was a nice enough young fella. His name was Mueller or Mollier or something like that. One day last week, I came in with a delivery and he just wasn't here. The guy before him was Jonathon Peach, a sort of short fat guy with too much energy. You know the type I mean. He had to be busy every second and when he talked, he talked really fast. Same thing happened with him. I came in and he was gone. The packages just keep piling up. Gotta go," he apologized, heading for the door. "See ya next week..." He paused, glanced back at Aleister with one raised eyebrow and a strange expression in his eyes. Then he changed what he had started to say. "I hope I'll see ya next week. Watch yourself around here. This is a strange place," and he was gone.

Aleister completed the application. He cautiously approached the table by the floor mirror and gently laid the papers on the table, as instructed. He turned to walk out the door, when he heard a rustling of papers. Looking back at the stack of papers he left on the table, he noticed a yellow Post It note on top of them. In large, bold handwriting, a message glared back at him. He leaned a little closer to see it. It said, **"Don't forget to SIGN the application, and stay away from the mirror."**

CƷ Ꝺ

He found his apartment just as he left it, with papers everywhere. The advertisement no longer flashed at him, but not only that, the advertisement for Flaass's clerical assistant had vanished. It just wasn't there. Reviewing the events of the explosion, the winged monkey and the strange experience in Flaass's office, Aleister wondered if it had all been a nightmare, a figment of his imagination. *This is crazy. I even thought I saw a winged monkey. Nothing in my apartment could have exploded, and nothing could be more bazaar than that floor mirror!* He doubted there would even be a fifth floor if he went back.

CƷ Ꝺ

Aleister grumbled to himself as he climbed the five stories to Flaass's office the next morning. The creaky wood stairway winding upward had an antiqued mahogany banister. The stairs groaned with each step. *This building must be a hundred years old.* He saw no one in the building at all, on either visit. The office doors he passed at the various landings all bore names of people in the literature business in one aspect or another. There, on the third floor "Pox" Merry Death had a sign in red and blue. *That rat. He charged me a four hundred fifty dollar reading fee then said my book was beyond redemption ... wooden characters without exception. And there's Beth Tomawda ... Tomayda/Tomawda. She took six months to get back to me with an unsigned, undated rejection letter. I don't even remember her reading fee. And there's Baines Literary on the fourth floor. He sent me an unsigned undated rejection letter with a handwritten scrawl saying he couldn't find the postage to return the actual manuscript. The letter was in my address-label-envelope with six dollars worth of postage on it. The goof.*

Conditioned by climbing to his fifteenth floor walk-up apartment, he found the fifth floor trek barely exerting. When he got to it, he found the heavy, wood door, as before, with the sign "Ronald M. Flaass Literary Agent." As he approached it, he heard the door unlock itself again. Inside, on the desk a nameplate exhibited his name, "Aleister M. Smiley, Clerical Assistant." Another delivery of manuscripts arrived since yesterday, stacked so closely to the back of the chair that he had to move it to pull the chair out to sit down. In the center of the desk rested another list of instructions. He nervously glanced around the room as he pulled on his latex gloves. The beautiful witch with the winged monkey in the painting watched him expectantly. The giant woman with the microphone winked at him again as he started pulling on the second glove. *This is too weird. Women in paintings don't wink. People don't sing or change places.* The people with the boxes on their heads had all moved from where they stood the day before. The now empty beer glasses stood on the top of the piano. This can't be, Aleister began mumbling to himself.

The instructions were very straight-forward, prefaced with, "Welcome to the Ronald M. Flaass Literary Agency. We place more books for publication than any other literary agency in New York. We're proud to have you working for us and you should be proud to be here. Your pay will be $.25 per minute of actual work time. We don't pay you to scratch your head, look at the paintings on the wall, cross your legs or blow your nose. After we learn to depend on you, you will be placed on salary and nose blowing will be included in your pay, but then you will have quotas you must meet to keep that stupendous salary we will offer you.

1. Stack the manuscripts in order of the 'received' dates.
2. Starting with the oldest one, open the package.
3. Remove the reading fee, check or money order.
4. Place the check on the distant right hand corner of the desk.
5. Pull one of our expertly written, unsigned, undated rejection letters from the stack on the stand beside the desk.
6. Place it in the return envelope.
7. If there is enough postage to return the manuscript, do that. If not, discard it in the garbage can on the other side of the desk. We sell them by the ton for recycling to toilet tissue.
8. Seal up the package to be returned to the aspiring writer and start a stack by the door so that the FEDUPS man can pick it up when he arrives.
9. Open the top, left-hand drawer of the desk and get out a deposit slip. As you remove the checks and money orders begin filling out the deposit slip.

10. As each deposit slip is completed, place the stack of checks with the deposit slip on the table beside the mirror.

"Peripheral duties:

"When the stack of unsigned undated rejection letters begins to get low, call the number on the bottom of the pile to order another ten thousand.

"Stay away from the mirror."

What! A! Ripoff! Aleister's mind raged. *All these people send all this money to have their manuscripts read and all he does is send it back and keep the money! And twenty five cents per minute. Let's see. At that rate, every four minutes I get one dollar ... if I don't scratch my head, pick my nose or cross my legs. This is sick.*

Suddenly, the room began to shudder. A hint of motion near the floor mirror caught Aleister's eye. He thought for a moment he saw a hand reach out of the mirror, but he wasn't sure. Of one thing he was sure: another Post It note appeared, stuck on the table beside the mirror. He went closer to read it. In bold hand writing the message said, **"This is the job. Take it or leave it."**

Aleister needed a job, however unusual it might be. He sat back down at the desk and reached for a manuscript, checked the date and began sorting. *I'm angry and I'm a writer. When I get angry, I get out my pen. I'll do that tonight.*

Something else had changed in the room. Aleister glanced around to try to figure out what. All the paintings hung in the same places. The office door remained closed, and the mirror in its place. Nothing seemed amiss, but there was something ... different. As Aleister worked, he gradually became aware of a small flashing, green arrow on the floor in front of the mirror. It pointed at the mirror, so faintly that Aleister couldn't quite be sure it was really there. So, he ignored it.

Sorting proved more interesting than he thought it would be. He kept coming across names he knew, like Stephen Duke from Bangor and John Crasham the retired attorney turned writer. On the bottom of one very old looking stack he even found one with the return address William Shakespeare, Stratford on Avon, England. *This place isn't that old*, thought Aleister. *Well, they could have moved, but is Flaass old enough...? No. That can't be. Maybe his dad was a literary agent, and his dad before him. That could be, but I don't think so. It couldn't go that far back.* Aleister neared the end of his first stack. It took most of the morning. When he got to a manuscript with the return label saying "Edmund Spencer," it proved too much for him. He returned to the desk and began opening and rejecting manuscripts. *I'll finish sorting these stacks of manuscripts tomorrow. Maybe.*

Most of the checks were for $250, some for $350 and some as high as $500. When he completely filled out one deposit slip, he clipped it to the checks listed on it, placed it on the table by the mirror and returned to his seat at the desk. He sat down and glanced at the table where he had just left the deposit slip and checks. It startled him to see the table was already empty except for another Post It note. This one said, ***"Keep up the good work."***

愈   愈

That evening he got together with his friend, Crystal Gooseworthy. Crystal wasn't anything like H'eung Yau, but she was beautiful to Aleister. She had long black hair, sparkling eyes and a ready smile. She filled out her regular uniform of a torn sweatshirt and faded jeans very nicely, in Aleister's candid opinion. "You went to work WHERE?!" she demanded. "That old crook Flaass has been solicited by every writer since John of Patmos. I never heard of anyone getting published through him. I don't know how he stays in business,"

"I do," said Aleister simply.

"And you told me one of the guys who worked there before you was Jonathon Peach? I know him. He used to show up at the Writer's Guild meetings in the Village." Her demeanor changed enough to make Aleister slightly jealous. "He wrote incredible poetry. I love to listen to him read it."

"Have you seen him lately?" asked Aleister.

"No," replied Crystal. "Not since... Oh my gawd. I heard he got a job with a literary agent. No one's seen him since."

愈   愈

Aleister's second day on the job started much like the first. Day jobs can be like that, but a few things occurred to break the routine. The FEDUPS man showed up with another stack of manuscripts and took away the ones Aleister finished packaging. The witch with the winged monkey smiled less broadly. The people with the boxes on their heads now seated themselves around a table to eat sandwiches. *Why do these paintings seem different every time I look at them? I mean, a painting is a painting. It stays the same century after century. I wonder if the people in these paintings visibly age.*

He brought two extra pairs of latex gloves with him today. On the first day, the pair he wore got smudged with ink. That offended him. Each time he placed a deposit slip on the table by the mirror, he grew more apprehensive about being near it. The flashing green arrow he could see on the floor gradually grew brighter. It glowed stronger than yesterday and he no longer refused to believe it to be real. It pointed directly at the mirror.

The day trudged on. While returning to the desk, after finishing the fourth deposit slip and placing it on the table by the mirror, he heard a slap behind him. He turned and found a letter-sized piece of paper lying on the table. He took it back to his desk, sat down and began to read. As he read, he grew quickly furious. It said,

Job Evaluation Summary

Although here nine hours yesterday, you are being paid for four hundred sixty six minutes (7 hours and 46 minutes). You perpetually scratched, shifted and rubbed at your ridiculous rubber gloves. You glanced perpetually at the paintings. You examined familiar names on address labels with far too much interest. You are simply going to have to work harder to achieve an offer of salaried employment.

It was signed by Mrs. Gertrude Flaass, executive director, Ronald Flaass Literary Agency.

Aleister grew livid. He rose from his seat, feeling the blood rushing to his face in rising anger. With his anger mitigated by fear, he straightened his shirt and brushed back his hair before marching to the mirror. In passing, he kicked a manuscript out of the way that burst open scattering pages everywhere. He stopped directly in front of the shimmering glass. His reflection revealed a disheveled young man, head slightly forward and fists clenched in readiness for a fight. His eyes flashed in anger and a faint layer of perspiration moistened his forehead. He paused in surprise for a moment because he saw nothing but his own reflection and it wasn't even a good quality mirror. *I don't know what I expected to see here. It's only a mirror, after all.* The image sort of shimmered as though the mirror needed to have its reflective coating refinished. Curious, he reached out to touch it, but his fingers went right through the shiny surface.

Suddenly, he felt a very strong hand grab his wrist and yank him toward the mirror. He expected to hear the shattering of glass, but he heard nothing except his breath being knocked out of him as he landed on some grassy turf in a large meadow.

Chapter 2: Never Ever Land

Aleister felt dazed. As his head stopped swimming, he noticed the shimmering wall, in front of him, the other side of the mirror. Through the mirror, his returning focus allowed him to see the office of Ronald Flaass. He tried to stand but got kicked back down by a big, beefy foot wearing a rubber flip-flop. For the first time, he saw a large woman standing over him.

"No one, and I do mean no one, goes back, once they know of this place," she announced menacingly.

"What is this place?" Aleister glanced around himself. The meadow ran on into the distance ahead. To the right, he saw a dense forest. To the right of the forest, a hedgerow almost as tall as the forest blocked his view. He could hear voices coming from beyond the hedges. A dirt path led from the shimmering wall toward the hedgerow, disappearing into it.

"This," the woman spoke slowly with what could not be mistaken as anything but great pride, "is Never Ever Land."

Aleister finally made it back to his feet and started toward the shimmering wall. The woman stepped in front of him and stiff-armed him violently, pushing him back three or four steps. He began eyeing her, assessing her. *If I charge her, maybe I could knock her over and get back through the mirror.* She reacted as though she could read his thoughts, bracing herself for the impact.

Aleister caught his breath as he took in her surreal stockiness. He guessed she stood at about five feet nine inches and weighed somewhere around two hundred fifty pounds. Matted, thin brown hair streaked with gray curls, loosely kept its form with the help of bobby pins. The pocked face looking down at him lacked adornment of any kind. Excessively long lobes retained large holes where heavy earrings must have once habitually dangled. A thick, truncated nose, overwhelmed by fat cheeks, poked out almost cautiously under bulging eyes that overshadowed her other features. They were dark and bloodshot with pin-point pupils.

Her low at the neck, sleeveless blouse barely concealed ponderously heavy appendages that heaved back and forth with her every movement. Her naked shoulders would have stood out on a Green Bay Packer. Black, cut-off shorts fell above the knee revealing legs muscular enough to drag a four-furrowed plow. As Aleister sized her up, she eyed him furtively, preparing herself for his next attempt to get back through the mirror. Aleister considered his hundred ten pounds and thought better of challenging her physically.

"Uh, may I ask who you might be?" he ventured politely, a bit fearful of sounding too ingratiating.

"I am Mrs. Gertrude Flaass." Her glare remained fixed on him. "I guard our gate, hire and fire clerical assistants and generally oversee the operation. I am my husband's office manager. Why couldn't you stay away from the mirror as I repeatedly asked? We hoped to keep you, but we can always find another. I've already sent the monkey to find your replacement."

So, the monkey was real? No. Just a minute, here. The monkey was not real and neither is this. This is some kind of weird hallucination. I must be losing my mind. He checked his latex gloves. Still there. Maybe this is real. "So you're telling me the winged monkey in my bedroom was really there. None of this makes any sense."

Mrs. Flaass guffawed, "The monkey certainly is real. We send him out to bring us writers who have real potential, to stop them before they get a legitimate chance for publication. Only Mr. Flaass gets published, if we can help it." She placed her fists on her ample hips, tossed her head in the air, (*a bit like a horse*, Aleister snickered to himself) and she continued with pride, "His books are wonderful. They're all written by computers and they all follow proven formulas. You know what I'm talking about." Her voice took on a conspiratorial tone. "The flawed and conflicted main character pursues a desperate cause, meets obstacle after obstacle, never managing to succeed until the very end and if then, only by accident or divine intervention."

"That's really unfair," protested Aleister. "But that explains why I keep getting the feeling that I'm reading the same book over and over when I buy new publications."

"It's very fair to us," she smiled demurely. "We make millions on this scam and there's nothing you can do about it because YOU are never ever going to leave Never Ever Land. No one leaves here who knows about it, except us. And no one who is here, ever gets published. Get it — yet?"

"I demand to speak with Mr. Flaass," declared Aleister angrily, returning her glare.

"Oh you shall. You shall, Mr. Smiley," she intoned menacingly. "Here he comes right now. "

Aleister looked in the direction of her gaze, toward the end of the path near the hedgerows. In the distance, he could see a very tall rabbit, but it walked rather than hopped toward them. "Is Mr. Flaass a rabbit?" he asked with sarcastic innocence.

"No," she practically snorted. "He thought it was funny to wear that childish rabbit costume. Your name is Aleister, right? You came through the looking glass, right? He was chortling all day yesterday about 'Aleister through the looking glass.' And he said, 'How can we have Aleister through the looking glass without a rabbit, a Cheshire cat and a chess game played by playing card characters?' "

"But that was Alice, wasn't it?"

"Of course it was Alice," she snapped. "But do you have any idea how hard it is to find aspiring writers named Alice who are dumb enough to accept the kind of job you took? He's obsessed with this nonsense." Her voice now took on the tones of a well-practiced recording. "Why, if it weren't for me..."

The man dressed as a rabbit drew near and Mrs. Flaass didn't want to be overheard. He towered over Aleister, easily six feet tall and with the rabbit ears, close to eight. The rabbit costume zipped up the front. Its design better suited the wearer to be on all fours, not walking upright, so it stretched oddly as he walked. Worse yet, the light blue outfit gave the impression of being a child's pajamas, made for an adult. Aleister watched in shocked dismay as Mr. Flaass came closer.

When he came within earshot, he stopped, smiled and greeted Aleister with, "Well, well, Mr. Smiley. I didn't think you'd last more than a day and I was right. I'm always right, you know. Now that we have you in Never Ever Land, I'm relieved that you will never ever be published and never, ever again have a chance at outshining my works. I've stopped you." He rocked back on his heels with obvious glee. If his rabbit suit had suspenders, his thumbs would, no doubt, have been hooked in them.

"Mr. Flaass," began Aleister, his anger rising again. "Don't you think that inundating the market with books written by formula stifles true creativity, cheapens the literature of our time and bores the desperate masses into watching things like baseball, football and basketball for their entertainment? If they HAD any good books to read, they'd never waste their time on such mindless pastimes. Now I know you are chiefly to blame for this abomination."

Flaass began sputtering, but before he could reply, Mrs. Flaass interjected, "You'd better take it easy on him if you know what's good for you, he can be very vindictive and unforgiving. Don't forget, Mr. Smiley, Mr. Flaass owns stock in thirteen football teams, twelve baseball teams, and thirty-two hockey teams."

Flaass so devoted himself to sputtering that he found himself unable to reply, immediately. *Maybe that's why,* thought Aleister, feeling a bit mean himself, *all his letters are unsigned and undated.* But Aleister already knew the reason for that.

"I must apologize." Aleister softened his tone. "I indeed didn't know that Mr. Flaass owns stock in sports teams. How rude of me to demean them." His sarcasm was obviously lost on Flaass. *Not the brightest star on the horizon, is he?* Aleister decided.

Flaass finally regained some of his composure. He glanced angrily at Mrs. Flaass, then furiously at Aleister. Then Flaass, once again playing the rabbit, ceremoniously pulled out a large pocket watch and recited, "I'm great. I'm great. I have no time to prate. No time to say reject because I'm great. I'm great. I'm great." With that, Mr. Flaass began hopping away toward the trees, but he stopped suddenly, only a few yards away. He turned back toward Aleister and snarled. "You'd better make yourself scarce, boy. If you're here when I get back, I'm going to send my Preditors after you. You'll be harried right into the ground, if you get my drift; rewrite after rewrite, for eternity, until the end." He turned and stalked off, this time toward the trees.

"Mrs. Flaass," Aleister turned toward the woman, trying to sound reasonable, "Please allow me to go home. Even if I told this story to others, no one would believe me."

"No," Mrs. Flaass sternly rejected the thought. "If you try again, I'll assign a winged monkey to follow you around to make sure you behave."

Aleister wrinkled his face in distaste and mimicked the words, "Winged Monkey? Isn't that a sort of mixed metaphor? I mean, if this is supposed to be *Aleister through the looking glass*, winged monkeys don't fit. Isn't that from *The Wizard of Oz*?"

"Listen, smart aleck," she snapped. "In Never Ever Land, we can steal anybody's ideas. That we've done that will never be known because, once here, a person Never Ever leaves."

"Mrs. Flaass," Aleister began trying again. "Did the winged monkey have anything to do with the explosion in my apartment?"

"We had to get your attention some how, didn't we?" She shrugged off the question.

Just then, they both turned at a sound coming through the shimmering wall. The door to Flass's office opened. A young woman entered wearing a torn sweatshirt and faded jeans. "Oh no," muttered Aleister. "It's Crystal Gooseworthy." *Has she come to visit me at work? Is she applying for a job? What's going on?*

"Oh good," oozed Mrs. Flaass. "We've replaced you already."

They watched in silence as Crystal seated herself at the desk and began filling out the application forms. "It's time for you to leave," announced Mrs. Flaass. "So, leave."

"Where can I go?" asked Aleister, reasonably. "I don't know anyone here except you. I have no idea where to go."

"Follow the path, fool. The only other direction is across The Endless Meadow. You'll starve before you get to the other side."

"What's on the other side of the Endless Meadow?" asked Aleister. "And why is it called that if there's another side to it?"

"No more questions, fool." Her face took on a very menacing expression. Her huge eyes narrowed and her lips drew themselves into thin, dark lines. She snapped her fingers and in the distance, high in the sky, Aleister saw a figure descending toward them. He quickly began backing away as it dawned on him, *It's a winged monkey!*

Aleister glanced around quickly and headed for the nearest cover, the forest. "Not a good choice, Smiley," he heard Mrs. Flaass behind him.

At the edge of the forest, the thick undergrowth along its edge stopped him. With another quick glance at the flying monkey still descending toward him, much closer now, he made up his mind. He ducked low, hoping to get under some of the thick brush and through it to the more open area of the forest just beyond, but before a moment passed, vines and stickers hopelessly tangled his ankles and legs bringing him crashing to the ground. The monkey landed a few feet away, just outside the thicket where Aleister lay trapped and he hoped, protected. He could hear a sound like chuckling. He remained motionless, trying to make himself invisible.

After a few moments, he could no longer hear the monkey chuckling but he remained silent and motionless, waiting to see if it had given up or found him. He practically held his breath in apprehension. More endless moments passed. Finally, Aleister could hear the flutter of wings. Assuming the monkey gave up and departed, he began examining just how he got himself so tangled. The vines wrapped themselves around his ankles and legs, as though they had done it intentionally. The vines trapped his left wrist against his chest. His right hand was free. Using it, he reached into his pocket and pulled out his pocket-knife. Struggling to get hold of the blade with the fingers of his trapped left hand, he managed to get it open. As the knife snapped open, he felt an immediate loosening of the vines around his chest, trapping his left hand. Finally able to move, he sat up. He reached toward his ankles with the intention of cutting the vines that imprisoned his legs, but he heard a soft voice that stopped him, saying, "Please, don't cut me."

"Who's talking to me?" Aleister demanded, nervously looking around.

"It's me, Bush," said the bush.

"I've never heard of a talking bush," replied Aleister in disgust.

"It's Bush, pal, not bush," the bush answered. "I was once a famous and powerful leader, depending on who you talk to. There I was in my office one day, when this shimmering, one-way floor mirror was delivered to me as a gift from Nancy Pelosi. Well. I guess you know the rest. I didn't know it was a one-way mirror until it was too late."

"I thought only aspiring writers were trapped here," ventured Aleister.

"That and anyone who Flaass grows to hate. He hated me because of my border policies. He thought it was amusing to turn me into a real bush and put me to work guarding his borders. My job here is to trap anyone who tries to pass, hold them till Flaass shows up and transmogrifies them into something that pleases him. He likes to turn people into things related to their names. My name is Bush, so, here I am. I'll be a vine till the end of time or until someone puts an end to Never Ever Land. I did this to myself because I argued with him about opening the borders between the real world and this one. Just think of it, I told him, free trade is good for everyone's economy."

"I guess it helps the poorer of the two who are trading," Aleister speculated. "It seems to me that it sort of brings them both to the same level. I think Flaass likes things the way they are here."

"Not altogether," moaned the bush. "He's a life member of the 'Roger Baldwin Litigation League.' Like them, he wants to put an end to private ownership of property, except for his own, of course. I argued with that idea and in his anger, he turned me into what I am today. Never confuse a literary agent with facts."

Aleister's feet were completely free by now, but suddenly he heard the flutter of monkey wings coming in. He began crawling toward the forest. "Be careful in there," cautioned the bush. "Almost every living thing you meet in this forest was at one time a free human being. The thing is that in time, they forget that and begin to believe they were always what they became here in Never Ever Land. Some are trees. Some are wildcats. Some are snakes, and you never ever know what they're going to do."

"How can I get home?" whispered Aleister, as the sound of a sickle cutting through the bushes reached his ears. "I mean how can I get out of Never Ever Land?"

"There's no way out that I know of," groaned the bush, obviously in great pain. "The birds who stop here sometimes talk of an Evil Queen somewhere in the east, but they never mention her name. They always call her 'you know who,' and 'she whose name cannot be mentioned.' They say if you go to her realm, it's the end, even, of Never Ever Land. What a horrible thought! You must hurry. They'll get to you soon if you stay here."

"Will you be alright? They're cutting you all up."

"Don't worry. I'm a natural outgrowth from stalwart roots. I'll grow back in time."

"If I continue into the forest, will I be able to find food? What's in there? Are there any other people who are really people or are they all converted plants and animals, like, uh, you?"

"You don't really have much choice. I heard what Flaass told you, that if he ever sees you again, you'll be sorry. When Flaass makes a threat like that, take it seriously. Many didn't, to their great regret. I heard Gertrude call you 'Smiley.' Is that your name?"

"Yes. Aleister Smiley."

"He'd probably turn you into a smiling Cheshire cat," the bush continued. "I heard him mention Cheshire cats, too. He probably thought a big smile too positive, though, for this place. He's not a very positive type of guy. He probably hates himself. He can't have any self-respect. Look at his life style. He's practically owned by that big woman and the only creative work he ever did was things like choosing that blue rabbit suit he's wearing. Now go. They're getting closer."

Aleister silently crept into the darkness of the forest. He glanced back over his shoulder and saw several winged monkeys tangled in the wide spread branches. It had their arms and wings wrapped tightly at their sides so they could no longer swing their sickles or fly to freedom. They began shrieking in rage, demanding to be released, but the bush just tightened its hold. "Hurry," he could hear it calling urgently to him. "Run!"

He headed deeper into the forest, running blindly. After he covered about a hundred yards, he turned ninety degrees to the right, and continued for another hundred. He kept going in that direction with the intention of zigzagging farther into the darkness when he saw light ahead, another end to the forest. He stopped, listening. Branches of nearby trees slowly reached toward him. He could hear soft voices all around him saying things like "Help me," and "Please wait."

How many people has Flaass trapped in here? How many are writers and how many could be people Flaass simply disliked? How will I ever get out of here?

Cʒ ᘔ

Crystal Gooseworthy feared the worst after her visit with "Al," as she thought of him. Because of his size, he always seemed so vulnerable and now he stuck himself in a job with that rotten crook, Ronald Flaass.

When she approached the door with the sign "Ronald M. Flaass, Literary Agency," she too heard the door unlock itself as she approached. The only difference in her experience of Flaass's office was the personal note signed by Gertrude Flaass, herself.

> *Dear Ms. Gooseworthy,*
> *We're so glad you're here. Our last assistant didn't stay very long and we are in desperate need of clerical help. Please provide the basic information we ask for and we hope you can consider starting immediately.*

It was signed Mrs. Gertrude Flaass, Office Manager.

Crystal wasn't as daunted by the mirror as Aleister. She knew what she looked like too and enjoyed looking at herself. She checked out the mirror before doing anything else, but when she tried to brush a fleck of dust off of its surface so she could see herself better, she was pulled directly through it. Mrs. Flaass was extremely angry.

"It is so hard to find clerical assistants who can follow instructions," she snarled as she shook Crystal by her arm. "You just wait here till Mr. Flaass arrives."

"Who are you?" Crystal demanded as she shook herself loose. "What is this place?"

When Flaass came hopping up in his rabbit suit, Crystal found herself shocked almost to silence. Almost. "What's with the rabbit pajamas?" She jabbed. "Blue, no less. I guess that's because you're a BOY? I thought literary agents were grown ups..."

That's as far as she got. Flaass began grinning demonically. Glaring at her, he raised his hand, frowning evilly. "Crystal Gooseworthy is it? Now, do I want a goose or a crystal? A crystal, I think. What kind of crystal should I make her Gertrude? I know. I always wanted a nice diamond ring. I'll make her a diamond.

Crystal began feeling very strange. Suddenly she was lying on the grass. Flaass approached her, bent over and picked her up. He held her up to his eye looking at her closely. "Not bad. Not bad, if I do say so myself," Flaass muttered as he placed the new ring on his finger. "I'll only wear it for a few days, Gertrude, then I'll give it to you if you wish? Would you like to be wearing this big diamond ring?"

"I think so, Ronnie. Diamonds are a girl's best friend."

Crystal started screaming. Flaass put his fingers in his ears. That really didn't help much because the act of bringing his hands close to his head brought Crystal that much closer to one of his ears. Finally, in desperation, he took off the ring and held it up in front of his face. Loudly he announced, "If you don't shut your mouth and keep it shut, I will turn you into a lump of coal and set you on fire. Is that clear?"

Crystal stopped screaming.

Chapter 3: The F'a Q

Arriving at the edge of the forest, Aleister discovered a large meadow. He knew this couldn't be the Endless Meadow, because he could see the other side of it. People of all sorts gathered, some of them wearing party hats. A few collected into a small group at one side of the meadow, to the left, and there entertained the others with musical instruments. Many just watched, while some sang along. To the right, along the other side of the meadow, a large canopy sheltered a picnic area. Several large tables pushed together, formed a long buffet and a procession of people stood waiting with plates in their hands. *FOOD!* Aleister's mouth watered. *And yes. I am hungry.*

In the center of the meadow a rotisserie turned slowly over a large fire. *Oh my gawd. What is that?* He walked closer, having to practically elbow his way in to get nearer to the fire and close enough to see. A large human figure rotated slowly on the spit. It wore thick, meat-ball glasses and looked just like a famous author from Bangor Maine. *What is his name? It's right on the tip of my tongue. Is it Queen? Prince? Duke? It's something like that. Monarch? Whatever.*

"Oh don't worry," chuckled a large mole standing next to Aleister. "It's a giant soy burger. We're eating him in effigy. We do this about once each week. Every time a writer gets published who becomes successful, Flaass orders what he calls an F'a Q. That's sort of short for an Effigy Barbecue. And no one's ever allowed to actually say their names. It's a sort of liability issue. Flaass is terrified of liability issues, but he still does this every week out of pure jealousy.

"Last week we ate someone from Newburg, New York. He writes formula detective novels. Flaass especially hates it when someone else is successful with formula works. They called the plates, 'plattersons.' I have no idea why."

Aleister observed this talkative mole with interest. He had never seen a talking mole before, but he was getting used to hearing things speak to him that couldn't normally talk. "Are you really a mole?" he politely inquired.

The mole looked up at him with small, doleful, myopic eyes. Aleister found the mole's act of looking up to be quite agreeable. Hardly anyone on Earth could look up at him. Aleister's height didn't permit that. Everyone looked down at him, but not this mole. This one stood quite tall, for a mole, almost five feet in fact, and it was standing on its hind legs. Its huge, front paws sported claws over six inches long and its nose actively tasted the smells on the air from the barbecue as it spoke. "Yes, but I wasn't always a mole," remonstrated the mole. "Flaass made me into a mole. He thought it was funny because my name is Le Molier. He laughed about making me a Lemming. I'm glad he didn't do that. I might have drowned by now. You can call me Leonard if you want. That's my first name."

As they joined the F'a Q's buffet line, Aleister took two paper plates and handed one to the mole, not quite sure how the mole would be able to handle it with those large claws and no real hands. He took it in both paws and when he needed to put something on the plate, he would lay the plate down. Once, when they got to the platters of sausages the mole called "little stevies," he put his plate down, ate three of them right then and there and grinning at Aleister, he put three more on his plate. They were like Swedish meatballs. When Aleister tried the first one, it was, justifiably, with great suspense.

Later at the picnic table, as they ate, Aleister asked, "Is there any way you've heard of, that we can get out of Never Ever Land?"

"No," the mole answered with resigned tones. "I've only heard rumors and innuendoes, but no one really knows and if they do know, they already left. One thing I have learned is that Flaass doesn't own the only mirror. There are numerous domains here. Each one is run by another literary agent or publisher and they all have their own mirror. But there is one idea I haven't been able to track down. There does seem to be a border. It's where 'you know who' lives. No one goes there." He continued eating.

"How does one get to the land of 'you know who?' "

"Oh, you don't want to go there," quibbled the mole. "She's evil. Everyone says so. She's the one behind this place, its inventor and keeper.

Without her, none of this would be possible."

"So," Aleister continued with fierce determination in his voice. "If 'you know who' is the inventor and keeper of Never Ever Land and without her none of this could be possible, then we need to eliminate her. If she's gone, then this place couldn't exist; right?"

The mole stopped eating. He looked up at Aleister in shocked realization and agreement. "You're right," he answered softly. "It could be dangerous. I don't know if I want to get involved with something like that. If Flaass found out, he'd have me for his next F'a Q."

Suddenly they heard loud voices followed by screaming. Before Aleister could even look around to see what was causing the disturbance, the mole grabbed him, half dragging him while he explained, "The winged monkeys are coming. Quick! Get under cover!"

Once safely in the forest and under a big clump of bushes, the mole explained while he quickly dug a burrow, "Flaass raids these parties if there's anyone he's looking for, and there's almost always someone, he's looking for."

Aleister watched in horror as two winged monkeys lifted off, carrying a squirming goat. Each of the two monkeys had a hold on one of the goat's horns. The goat was bleating pitifully and trying to kick at the monkeys. With a jolt, Aleister realized this was an unusual looking goat. It was wearing horned rimmed glasses. He glanced around the meadow trying to see if any more winged monkeys were still there.

"Keep down," advised the mole. "There are usually six or eight of them. Once they land, if they can't find who they're looking for, they sort of lay low, waiting for the rest of the people to come out of hiding. It won't be safe to come out again till well after dark, if then. Come on down in the burrow I just dug. We'll be safe there." The mole started chuckling and added, "Flaass had no clue that when he made me a mole, I'd be able to dig a burrow and successfully hide from him."

"Who is the goat?"

"One of Flaass's old teachers, I think, by the name of Askey, I think algebra or geometry. Flaass is very vindictive. If you cross him, he'll get you sooner or later, if he can. And one more thing about those winged monkeys, sometimes they'll hide and spy on things. Then a little later the Preditors will come in and ferret out anyone hiding that the monkeys can't get to. You need to come down in my burrow with me. If the Preditors show up, we can cover up the entrance till they go away.

The meadow seemed deserted. The canopies sheltering the tables and buffet line flapped gently in the evening breeze. The place had the appearance of being completely deserted, but Aleister remembered what the mole told him about the monkeys possibly hiding somewhere.

Without moving a muscle or revealing himself from under the bush, he surveyed the meadow area, looking for anywhere they might be able to hide. In the far end of the meadow, he thought he saw a green light flashing. *Oh no. Another arrow? I wonder if it's Flaass who puts those where I'll find them.* Aleister silently crept backwards till he felt the edge of the mole's burrow. Hating the dirt on his latex gloves, clothes, hair and face, he slid down into the hole in the Earth.

"Come further in," whispered the mole. "I'll close the entrance. We'll be safe down here. When the Preditors come, we'll be able to hear them clearly and we'll know when they've left. You'll see."

Who is this mole? Can I trust him? He wants me to crawl into a hole in the ground that he dug and then close it in. I'm not a mole. Can I survive in a closed hole in the ground? "Is there enough air? Won't I suffocate in a closed up hole like this?" he finally asked the mole as he slid down into the ground.

"Gee, I don't know." The mole pondered the question. "I never have, but I'm mole. I'll tell ya what. I won't close the hole completely. I'll leave it open a little bit so we can be sure to have air circulation."

The sounds of heavy footsteps seemed to vibrate through the ground. "We need to close it completely if only for a short time," the mole tossed over his shoulder as he hurried toward the entrance. "They're almost here."

Suddenly, what little light was left of the fading evening, vanished. Aleister could hear the sound of the mole digging more, then rustling around. "What ARE you doing?" At that moment, a light appeared, revealing the walls of the hole around them. To Aleister's surprise, the mole was holding a sort of lamp he had fashioned from a large snail shell. Inside the burrow, two short bunks and a low table now adorned their makeshift cave. The ceiling wasn't high enough for Aleister to stand up, but he could sit up with plenty of headroom. The mole found Aleister's look of surprise amusing.

"I'm not a total rodent. Not yet," he softly explained. "We'll be safe here, till they go away."

ᴄ₰   ᴔ

Aleister woke with a start. He dreamed he was buried alive under mountains of rejection letters from publishers all over the world. Most of them said they didn't accept un-agented submissions. When he opened his eyes, all he saw was darkness. The mole heard him moving around and opened the way to the surface. Morning had come.

Aleister could see no one in the meadow. He looked in the direction where he thought he had seen the flashing green light the night before. Nothing seemed unusual. Exiting the hole in the ground they began walking across the meadow to where the flashing green light had appeared. It surprised Aleister to find that some of the canopies along the edge of the meadow sheltered shelves of books with price tags on them. He walked over to one of the bookshelves and began browsing. The mole took a seat on the ground nearby and watched with a sardonic smile. Aleister picked up the first book. Its title was *How to Get Published,* by Ronald M. Flaass. Aleister opened the book to the first page. It started, "Once upon a time..." Aleister closed the book and put it back on the bookshelf. He picked up a second book, one from the next bookshelf. This one was titled, *Editing Guide For the First Time Author,* by Ronald M. Flaass. He opened this one to its first page, too. It started out "It was a dark and stormy night..." Aleister put the book down and turned in frustration to look for the mole. It still sat in the meadow, laughing quietly.

"What did you expect to find in Flaassland?" chortled the mole. "His computer is the author of every one of those books. Flaass is too busy playing at being a rabbit to write books. And you know what they say about computer generated books. They're like government — money in, garbage out."

Ignoring the mole's mirth, Aleister walked a little closer to him and said, "Last night I saw a flashing green light over there in the corner of the meadow. In my apartment, I saw a flashing green light before I applied for the job at Flaass's office and then again on the floor of the office pointing toward the mirror. The arrow is part of the reason I got so close to the mirror in the first place. Have you seen anything like that?"

"Yes I did," the mole answered, "but every time I followed them, I got into more trouble. So, I quit. I haven't seen one in a long time."

"Well," began Aleister. "I've been thinking. I don't believe Flaass put those flashing green arrows where I could see them. I don't know what they are, why they're there or who is behind it, and I don't know if that person has evil intent toward me or not."

As he said this, he fingered the thumb drive that still hung around his neck. Three manuscripts he had written were on that thumb drive. No one knew it was there but him and he planned to keep it that way.

"I do know, that I am going to continue searching for the person everyone calls 'you know who' and if what you said about her is true, I am going to end Never Ever Land and go home. No matter what it takes." As he said this, Aleister furrowed his brows, narrowed his eyes and clenched his teeth in determination.

౮ ಜ

The mole, now quite close, saw the grit appearing in Aleister's expression and through that determination of Aleister's, remembered his own hopes and dreams for a better life through the publication of his own works. He remembered Flaass's words, "We send the monkeys out to find writers who have real potential, to bring them to us and trap them here so that they Never Ever get published." The mole remembered his rush of joy when he realized that through Flaass's magic, he learned that the name of Le Molier had "real potential." He watched as Aleister glowered at him, waiting to hear if he was coming along on this quest of sorts, or not. Something stirred in the mole that had not stirred in a long, long time. He remembered his mother and father whom he had not seen in weeks, maybe months. He remembered a girl he liked with long black hair named Crystal Gooseworthy and the dreams he had for a better life, perhaps with her. The mole rose on his hind feet. He brushed the loose dirt from his hide. He twitched his short cars, wriggled his nose testing the wind and said, "I'm coming with you."

ଔ ଛ

Together, the two marched to the end of the meadow and began searching for signs of flashing green arrows. They found none. Instead, they discovered a path leading toward the east and the rising sun. Shortly along the way, it divided into three new paths. Signs pointed in their various directions with labels that said, "Boxland, 17 miles," and "Shrewsberryland Academy of Learning, Shrewsberryland, 12 miles." The third sign read, "Filthydelphia, 362 miles."

Aleister stopped and observing the signs, he scratched his head and mumbled, "Which is the path less traveled by? That might make all the difference, you know?"

"They all look equally worn to me," groaned the mole. "And I don't think that following that old poem is necessarily a good guide in these circumstances. Do you?"

"What other guidance do we have? I see no flashing arrows and I never heard of any of these places. Although Shrewsberry sounds vaguely familiar, Shrewsberryland doesn't. And Filthydelphia, I think is in Mississippi or Pennsylvania, but we aren't in either of those places. And what's Boxland? It sounds like a place where there are a lot of aluminum mines. What do they call that stuff, bauxite? Well considering this place, that could be a misspelling."

"There are only two of us," noted the mole. "So if we vote on it and we disagree, there will always be a tie vote. How can we decide?"

"Ahem," stated a cultured sounding voice of resonant quality. "May I be of assistance in some way?"

Aleister and the mole looked around earnestly, both having thought they were alone. Neither noticed the roundish shaped rock, lying beside the path. It had strange markings on it, a sort of serrated edge, and a trail in the dirt behind, revealing that it had motivated itself to this particular location, if rather slowly. Aleister and the mole looked at each other and the mole said, "I don't see a thing. Do you?"

"I don't see anything, either," Aleister replied. "Who are you and where are you?" Aleister directed his question to the universe in general.

"I know my camouflage does well to conceal me from the Preditors, but at times it can be inconvenient. I am on the ground, slightly to your right."

They both looked down to the right. They both saw the roundish rock and as they spotted it, four legs popped out in appropriate locations, followed by a tail at one end and a head at the other. The tortoise looked up at them and announced, "I would be delighted to smile in greeting, but the beak on this face is quite inflexible. You may call me Lawrence, if you wish. I have gathered that you two fellow travelers are in a quandary for a correct decision. What do you seek?"

The mole looked at Aleister and Aleister looked at the mole. Almost simultaneously, they said to one another, "Can we trust him?"

The tortoise slowly moved his head, eyeing each of them carefully. Painstakingly, he lifted his mass on his four legs and turned to face them more directly. He cleared his throat again, "Ahem." Then he said almost as an announcement, "In this forest, we are all like passengers in a small boat, tossed on a stormy sea. We owe one another a terrible loyalty. Trust here is a necessity. In other places, it is a function of serendipity. Choose, and I will help you if I can."

"Lawrence," opened Aleister, assuming correctly the agreement of the mole. "We seek the home of 'you know who.' "

"Ahem," coughed the tortoise redundantly. "I believe it's 'you know whom,' is it not?"

"Let's not quibble about syntax," snorted the mole irascibly. "Do you know where she lives, or not?"

"Syntax is incredibly important," announced the tortoise. "Don't you realize that more manuscripts are returned for poor syntax than for any other reason? 'Dialect,' they say. 'Regional usage' they say. 'Colloquialism,' they say. It's all euphemisms and justification for poor syntax."

"You're absolutely right," Aleister politely replied. "Syntax is incredibly important. Do you know the way to the home of she who cannot be named?"

"Yes," said the tortoise. "But the path is long and laden with many dangers. Why do you choose such a path? And thank you for saying it correctly."

Aleister and the mole again shared a look. They both rolled their eyes. The mole turned his back on the situation to conceal his grin and Aleister turned again to the tortoise. "Our life's purpose has led us to seek this path, and we must find it. Do you know which path it is? If you do, please tell us. The day wears on."

"Your impatience is typical of those who are fleet of foot. Slow and steady is my motto. A chapter a day, that's the way. No more. No less. No more. No less. Why do you seek such a deadly passage? Without this information, I will surely not tell."

"But I will. I will," shrilled a voice from overhead. Aleister and the mole both looked up. A mockingbird circled above them. As they spotted it, it landed on the twig of a large tree with branches overhanging the path.

"He doesn't know," muttered the tortoise. "He's just a twit."

"Judge ye not," quoted the mockingbird in the tortoise's voice. "I've flown there many times," it continued in its own voice. "How many times have you crawled there from here, turtle? Do you even know the answer to their question?"

"Oh, I know," intoned the tortoise. "Guard her lair. These two look murderous."

"She can protect herself well enough," tweeted the bird. "She's the Queen of the East Gate." The mockingbird lifted off the twig where it had landed. It flitted around the intersection of paths and lighted directly on the back of the tortoise. The tortoise snapped at the bird, but couldn't reach it.

"You tease me sorely," the tortoise warned. "Someday, you may come too close."

"If you need to reach the lair of 'you know who,' " began the mockingbird.

"Whom!" roared the tortoise.

"You must take the path through the village of the Boxheads," continued the bird. "You must not stay there long. Sleep, before you enter their village, and go directly through, leaving as soon as possible. It's not a safe place for a visit. Keep traveling east from Boxland and you will eventually get there."

"How could you tell them?" demanded the tortoise. "You don't know them. They could be from Flaass or one of those other idiots."

"If she's so evil, why do you object?" asked Aleister. "Are you an emissary of that evil? Perhaps we should kill him too?" Aleister directed his question to the mole.

The tortoise's head, legs and tail shot back into its shell. "Go ahead and try," they heard its voice, echoing from inside its shell.

"Leave it," the mole turned to go. "He's just another one of Flaass's victims. Let's move on. I believe the mockingbird."

The path began descending. It went round and round rocky turns passing promontory after steep cliff. In the distance, they soon spotted a river with a town on both sides surrounding a bridge. They approached cautiously and when they began to see homes on both sides of the road, they decided to retreat a few hundred yards and find a safe place to sleep under the trees of the forest. Their burrow for the night was just behind a sign that said, "Welcome to Boxland."

Chapter 4: The Land of the Box-Heads

First light in Box Land revealed a terrain that could only have been created by a cubist painter. Oblongs overran squares and more oblongs. Even the plants sported squared off stems and leaves. Aleister heard a sort of "thump, thump, thump," accompanied by the sound of whistling. He turned to see a bicyclist riding a contraption with square wheels. Actually, the wheels were a square overlapping a square so that the wheel had eight points instead of being round. The points of the wheels striking the road caused the sounds and Aleister could hear more coming in the distance. That two wheels did this, resulted in sixteen points striking the ground with each revolution of the wheels, if one could call them wheels. *Maybe I should call them octagons?* Aleister mused.

The mole, standing beside Aleister, scratched his head with one of those long claws, yawned and asked, "I wonder why that bicyclist is wearing a box on his head?" The mole paused. He yawned again and added with a sort of wonder in his voice, "Maybe I should have said octa-cyclist?"

Looking at the oddly shaped wheels, or octagons so consumed Aleister that he failed to notice the box on the rider's head, completely concealing his face from view. Only the rider's mouth remained visible under the opening of the box. "How can he see where he's going with that box on his head?" Aleister smiled at the chorus of thumping as more octagon wheeled bicycles appeared from around the bend. "Look. Here comes another one, and more behind that one. It looks like a commute to work or something like that."

The two watched in amazement, as the many octa-cyclists passed them on the road toward town. The turns in the road didn't curve, of course. Each turn described a perfect, ninety-degree angle. The octa-cyclists skillfully completed each ninety-degree turn without running off the road or running into each other.

"Let's get through here as quickly as we can." Aleister's demeanor turned more serious as he cautiously watched riders. "This place is crazy."

"We better be pretty careful if we're walking along the roadway. I don't think these characters can see where they're going."

"There's no need for them to see," a nearby voice chimed in. "They learned this road before they were ten years old. It hasn't changed any, so there's no need for them to actually see it again. Everything we adults need to know is inside the boxes on our heads."

Aleister and the mole both started. Watching the octa-cyclists so consumed them, they failed to notice this pedestrian. A teen-aged girl with a box on her head now approached. She stopped and waited for a reply with her hands on her hips. Blonde hair cascaded out from under the box, spilling down over a pink blouse with square shoulders, box-pleated skirt and square-toed sneakers.

"You must not be from around here," the girl continued, "or you would know all this. Don't worry, when you get to town, if you mention it to anyone, one of the Angle-Cops will help you get your own boxes. TTFN," she added with a giggle.

"TTFN?" pondered the mole.

Aleister rolled his eyes, shook his head and muttered, "Oh pooh. That stands for 'ta ta for now.' Let's get moving. With a little luck we can be out of here before noon."

"Agreed," the mole muttered in resignation.

The buildings grew closer together as they neared the city proper. They could see small office buildings, churches and cubist graffiti on the sides of the buildings and in the alley-ways. The church architecture expressed cubist rapture with cube shaped domes and square bells. The squared off tops for the stained glass windows replaced the traditional dome shapes. Their art virtually defined its own version of Extreme Cubism. Aleister and the mole started snickering when they approached a town park bearing a sign in front saying "The Town Square."

A small crowd assembled in front of an outdoor platform chatted among themselves waiting for some event to begin. On the stage, two microphones silently waited for their speakers. A sign above the stage announced the "Square Land Pride, Annual Debates (held every four weeks on an annualized subject)." The sign went on to explain, who today's contenders were to be. Dr.Helmut Tilkey headed the list. Posters standing near the stage identified him as the submitter of the Gorlitzer Prize winning manuscript titled *Thinking Within the Box*. His contender already sat waiting just off stage. Today, the posters said, it would be Dr. Dietrich Braunhoffer, Professor of Concentric Religious Studies at Boxheart University of Flaass's Bleeding Heart and author of numerous prize-winning manuscripts on the subject of *Square Root Theology*.

"How do these people read these signs with boxes on their heads?" Aleister wondered out loud. The mole just rolled his eyes in reply.

"Do you want to stay and listen to the debate?" Aleister whispered to the mole.

"No," the mole whispered back. "Let's get out of here."

As they began slipping away toward the bridge and the road leading east, out of town, Aleister felt a hand on his arm. He turned to find a policeman wearing a box on his head with two holes cut out so he could see. "Where are you two going?" asked the policeman. "Attendance at these debates is mandatory. By the way," the policeman continued, "why aren't you two wearing your boxes?"

"Uh, we, uh..." began Aleister

"We just arrived in town," the mole interjected. "We were hoping to encounter an officer so we could inquire about how to get boxes. Is there somewhere we can go for an appointment or application?"

"You're out of luck today," answered the policeman. "The head-bolt maker has been sick and we ran out of head-bolts yesterday."

"Head bolts?" stammered Aleister.

"Of course," replied the policeman matter-of-factly. "The boxes are all bolted to peoples' heads so that they don't fall off while they're riding their octa-cycles to work and back, or if they have a fall. We have a lot of falls here. People just can't seem to remember where they're going."

"Remember where they're going?" repeated Aleister incredulously.

"Certainly," answered the policeman as though this were the simplest matter on Earth. "They obviously can't SEE where they're going, so they have to remember. Timing is important too, especially on the octa-cycles. In Box Land, everyone learns all they need to know, by the time they're thirteen years old. After that, it's all repetition, but you already know that."

"May I ask you a question?" Aleister was examining the box on the policeman's head.

"Of course, you may. Ask away."

"I noticed that you have holes cut in the front of the box on your head so that you can see. I haven't seen holes in anyone else's boxes.

Why do you have holes?"

The mole took a deep breath, obviously wishing he could vanish somewhere. He began looking wistfully at the ground. Aleister knew he was looking for the right place to dig a burrow for a quick escape, if necessary.

"All policemen have eye holes. How else could we know if everyone is obeying the box law? It's a natural part of our box-acracy. But, of course, we only look out through those holes when it's absolutely necessary. Everything we need to know or think about is inside the box. You'll learn. We have a very good orientation program. It's called 'Box Law for Wearers of Other Hats.'"

Searching for any avenue of escape, the Mole noticed a bookstore cross the street. In front of the bookstore stood a large dumpster. A clerk from the bookstore working at filling it with partially empty book boxes paused to listen to their conversation with the Angle-Cop. On each visit to the dumpster, he dropped more book boxes into it, paused to listen and returned for more trash.

"I have a wonderful idea," the mole interrupted the conversation. "Can we borrow a couple of used boxes from the bookstore and wear those till tomorrow when we can get our very own boxes bolted to our heads?"

The policeman looked at the bookstore, then at Aleister and the mole. He glanced around the crowd to see if anyone had heard this suggestion, then he said, "That would look better for me. If by some strange chance, someone else noticed you two thinking around outside your boxes, I could get in trouble. That way you won't have to be locked up till tomorrow and you'll be free to enjoy the debates and our wonderful Box Land. But don't forget, tomorrow at 0800, you must come to the office and sign up for your boxes and orientation. The office is right over there." He pointed toward a square brick building with bars in the window. "I'll see you there. Okay?"

"Great," Aleister promised. "We'll be there."

"That'll be fine," agreed the mole. "We'll just run over to that dumpster and get our boxes."

Aleister couldn't just take the boxes from the dumpster. He had to check out the books that were being thrown away, and there were lots of books. The first one he picked up, titled *How to Profit by Thinking Inside the Box*, listed its author as Ronald M. Flaass. The second one displayed the title *The Road to Health and Wealth Through Internalizing Aggression*. The author it listed was also R.M. Flaass. "This is pretty amazing," remarked Aleister. "How can anyone read a book with a box on his head anyway?"

"Maybe that's why they're throwing them away. No one buys them," the mole snickered.

The policeman watched to make sure they returned to the debate, so they were stuck with returning to it. Obviously, no one wanted to be there, but with mandatory attendance and angle-cops everywhere, they had no choice. The volume of the voices in the crowd grew with their restlessness at waiting. The mole, a little more agitated than usual, insisted that they work their way toward a large clump of bushes, pruned in a square shape, growing under a large, boxwood tree. When they got to it, the mole whispered, "Wait here and try to not let the Angle Cop see under the bush behind you." He then disappeared under the bush.

Dr. Braunhoffer rose to speak first. His poorly concealed girth tightly stretched a gray suit and vest, both unbuttoned. A long, gray, beard and gray hair protruded out from under the box on his head and the box displayed his logo on all four sides that read, "R2." Hanging his thumbs on his belt accentuated his portly stature. He loudly cleared his throat in preparation for speaking. As he approached his microphone, the crowd applauded.

What's that mole up to? Aleister wondered enviously. *I bet he's dug himself a nice hole and he's taking a nap. He's got the right idea, I guess.*

Braunhoffer took a deep breath, about to begin to speak, but before he finished clearing his throat, he grabbed onto the microphone stand and toppled over to his left. Aleister noticed that all the seats on the stage with their various dignitaries all slid in the same direction. The stage to Aleister's right was collapsing. The two posts supporting it slowly sank into the Earth giving an increasing tilt to the stage. As it sank, the people on the stage slid faster until they piled upon each other in the grass at the edge of the platform. Aleister watched in amazement. They were crying out in surprise and confusion, "Help! Help!"

The official trying to help people get to their feet wore the same box as the angle-Cop policeman, they spoke with earlier. "Moles!" Aleister could hear him shouting. "This was caused by moles!" The policeman began looking around the crowd, trying to find them. He had just spoken with a mole not long before. The mole popped out of the ground behind Aleister. After placing the box back on his head, he came out from under the bush, nudged Aleister and suggested, "Let's disappear with the rest of this crowd."

If they stayed in the midst of the crowd, the boxes on their heads would blend with all the other box-heads leaving for their homes. For all practical purposes, the boxes on their heads kept them invisible to the Angle-Cop as long as they stayed in the crowd.

The tiny holes Aleister cut in his box with his pen knife made it possible for him to see where he was going. He could still hear the policeman shouting about moles, but the voice sounded fainter and more distant. The crowd moving across the bridge kept up a leisurely pace. "Smooth move, mole," whispered a voice behind them.

A young man in a red shirt and pinpoint holes poked in his box so he could see paced them close behind. "I saw you come out of the hole under the bush. It was you that sunk the speakers' stand. Wasn't it? Thanks for doing that. No one wants to go to those stupid debates. We've all heard those guys argue dozens of times. No one's going to miss hearing it again."

"No problem," the mole answered with a smile. "We were in sort of a hurry to keep moving."

"Yeah, man," another young voice joined in. "We saw you get the boxes out of the dumpster. Way to go. We know you're not from around here. We thought we were going to have to, like, rescue you from Officer Opie."

"We pull stuff on Opie all the time," yet another voice added. "I bet he thinks we did that to the speakers' stand."

"How many of you are there?" Aleister tried to encourage them to provide more information. *I wonder if they can be recruited to help fight the evil queen?*

"Oh. Sorry, man," one of them answered quickly. "That's a secret. We have a very illegal club. We call ourselves the Box Lighters because light can get into all of our boxes."

"And we can, like, see out of them," explained another. "I think we're the only ones in Box Land who know why those dudes get prizes for manuscripts instead of for publications. It's because this is part of Never Ever Land. No one ever actually gets published here."

"Flaass gets published," added the guy in the red shirt.

"Yeah man, but like, he, like owns the place. And no one here reads his stuff or anything else for that matter. No one can read because they can't see outside of their stupid boxes."

"So, why don't you just take the boxes off?" asked the mole quite reasonably.

"Tradition, man," came the answer. "We've been wearing boxes like, forever."

"Comes a time," pontificated the mole, "to start thinking outside of the box."

"Yeah man," they all started laughing. "That's what we've been tryin' ta' tell people, but hey man. Here, it's like, super illegal to even talk like that."

"Last year, man," began another. "We got caught in a big rain storm at the debates. Everyone's boxes got all soggy and fell off. You should have seen how upset they were that they could see outside their tiny little world of blindness. Some of them got mad and denied that what they saw was real. Some of them went crazy. My mom was sick for more than a week. They had to put her back through orientation to get her straightened out."

"For some, it was the first time they had seen outside their boxes since they were, like, kids," another interjected.

"Most people just like to stay sequestered in their own little worlds, I guess," the mole complained. "They really don't care what's going on in the world around them. That's sort of scary when you consider that many of them vote. If we're not careful, boxes on our heads could be mandated everywhere."

Aleister started chuckling. "Flaass would back a movement like that, as long as he has his little make believe world behind his looking glass where he can play at being a blue rabbit."

"It doesn't seem too make-believe, just now." The mole tipped his box up so he could have a quick look around. "If it were make-believe, when we woke up this morning we'd have been in our own beds, instead of in that burrow I dug in the meadow. It seems to me that I'm still a mole. I don't know how you escaped without being changed into something. You were lucky."

Aleister and the Mole steadily climbed the hill toward the eastern edge of the town. The houses along the side of the road now watched over sizable farm tracts. Their companions gradually disappeared along the way to go to their homes. "Do you think," Aleister began. "That we might be able to recruit some of that club to help us with the evil queen?"

"No I don't." The mole paused a moment and shook his head. "They're just kids. By the time they're old enough to do something like that, they'll be as programmed as their parents and terrified to look outside their boxes."

They had reached the edge of town. A sign stood before them saying, "You are leaving Box Land."

Chapter 5: The Land of the Black and Whites

Aleister searched his pockets frantically for a fresh set of latex gloves. Trying to rinse the dirt off his filthy hands without soap frustrated him. The stream at the edge of the road presented itself handily but the lack of soap made his efforts useless. He had been in Never Ever Land for days without a shower or change of clothes. *This is getting tiresome,* he fumed. *How long is it going to be till I get out of here? Maybe it would have been better if Flaass had changed me into a mole, too. The mole looks as fresh every day as the day before. He doesn't seem to miss showering. Moles don't shower, I guess. Sleeping in a hole in the ground doesn't help me much and food is becoming a problem. Here it is mid morning and I haven't had anything to eat. I wish I could get published, then I wouldn't have had to go to work for people like Flaass and I'd not be hungry. At least with this experience I now know that it's impossible to get published unless I become a literary agent or a publisher, myself. Who would have thought, but then... How do famous writers like Stephen King do it? Wait a minute. He writes formulas too. Maybe, computers generate his books, too. I'll have to look into that, but first, I have to get out of Never Ever Land.*

No truer thing had he yet thought.

The overcast morning sky promised rain. The mole grutzed continuously in the ground near the road, looking for bugs or roots or what ever disgusting things it is that moles eat. Aleister glanced around the area. *Wish I had taken that YMCA Wilderness Survival course.* He didn't know where to look for food and he was hungry. He spotted a cultivated field across the stream behind a barbed wire fence. *Hmm. What's growing over there?*

He found a spot in the stream where he could work his way across without getting his feet wet. Very carefully, he picked his way across the stream stepping on rocks and limbs lodged among them. Climbing the other side of the bank toward the fence, he slipped on its wet sides twice, sliding back into the creek. Finally, making it to the top, he stopped next to the barbed wire fence. Now, how to cross the fence and get some food without getting his clothes or his skin torn on the barbed wire? *But what are they growing? Is it ripe enough to eat some of it?* Then he saw them. Nicely formed cantaloupes peeking out at him from under the broad leaves of their vines. *Yes,* thought Aleister, *reaching into his pocket for his knife.*

He stretched out on the ground on his back, lifted the bottom string of wire and slid under the fence. A moment later he was sitting amidst the cantaloupe plants with the sweetest one he had ever tasted. Suddenly he heard a deep-throated voice behind him saying, "Don't you move a muscle. You thief."

He slowly turned to look and what he saw confused, amazed and terrified him. He didn't know which to fear more, the shotgun in his face or the odd looking man holding it. About as tall as Aleister, five feet seven inches, the man's stockiness presented an almost perfect square of human flesh and it appeared to be all muscle. The man wore a heavy, cotton plaid shirt of red, white and green. That was partly concealed by bulky farmers' blue denim overalls. The floppy straw hat on the man's head half concealed his face, so Aleister couldn't quite be sure if the man's face was half black and half white or if it was an illusion caused by the shadows under his hat. Aleister glanced quickly at the man's hands and sure enough, his right hand was white and his left hand was black. It wasn't the pink or tan white of a Caucasian man but a pasty dead white, like white typing paper. The black wasn't softened with a little brown like a black man but was the solid, flat, black of bituminous coal.

This discovery didn't distract Aleister from the shotgun for very long. He didn't have time to worry about the man's unusual coloring or the way he dressed. He heard the order and saw the threat of the firearm. Softly he answered, "I'm sorry, mister. I was just so hungry and I saw these wonderful cantaloupes. I'll be happy to pay you for it, or work for it. And I did just take only one. It's not like I was cleaning out the field to go and sell them."

The man slowly lowered his weapon. He pulled off his straw hat revealing a mop of black and white hair that matched his face and hands. With a handkerchief he wiped the perspiration from his face. Putting his hat back on, he replied, "You shouldn'ta come in here at all. This is private property. Howdja git in here anyway?" The man's scowl deepened. "Didja cut ma' fence?"

"No sir," replied Aleister. "I slid under it."

"I wondered howya gotcher backside sa' dirty. Why doncha come along to the house an' have some proper breakfast? We'll hep ya git cleaned up a bit."

Aleister was half way to his feet when the man startled and raised the shotgun again. This time he pointed it toward the fence. Aleister followed his gaze and saw that the man now pointed the gun at Leonard the mole. "I ain't never seen such a big mole," the man's voice was muffled in concentration as he drew a bead on Leonard Le Molier. "We don't need no moles."

"Please stop," Aleister almost choked on his urgency. He was trying not to raise his voice too much, trying not to alarm the farmer any more than he had already. "That's not a mole. That's a writer by the name of Leonard Le Molier. Ronald Flaass turned him into a mole. He thought it was funny because of his name. Please don't shoot him."

"Is he with you?" the farmer accused him loudly.

"He is but he's not on this side of the fence," Aleister pointed out. "He already had his breakfast. He eats roots and bugs and things that moles eat. We're trying to get out of Never Ever Land so he can be turned back into a man."

The farmer lowered his weapon again, with an even deeper frown. "So izzy a mole or not?"

"Well, he's a mole for now, but inside that mole skin he's a man. Ask him. You won't find many moles that can talk and think like a human."

"Are you a mole or not?" demanded the farmer of Leonard.

"Please don't shoot me," pleaded the mole. "I'm a writer that Ronald Flaass changed into a mole. My name is Leonard Le Molier. I'm traveling with Aleister there. We're trying to find a way out of Never Ever Land."

"Well, I'll be." His tone softened as he lowered his shotgun. The farmer removed his hat and scratched his head. "I never seen a mole that could talk before. If you promise to not dig in my ground, I'll let you come along and feed ya with the other one. I never seen a mole that could walk on its hind legs, neither."

The way to the farmer's house led over hill and dale. *This farm must be huge.* Aleister could see field after field, rolling into the distance. *There's wheat. Over there is corn. I wonder if he has the really good stuff, the Bodacious Corn, that the Weavers grow in Pennsylvania.* He passed over another hill and spotted potatoes. *Gawd. What can't he grow here?*

The farmer chatted away as they walked. "My name is Wayland Zimmerman. Y'all can call me Wayland if you want. Y'all know, when you crossed the creek back there, you left Flaassland. This is Bethland. This is Beth Tomawda's domain. She's the 'Fat Lady' that everyone talks about. You know what I mean. They say 'it's over when the fat lady sings.' Well Beth is the fat lady. If you make it to the Valley of The Shadow of Beth, you'll see what I mean."

"Is that east of here?" the mole wanted to know. "That's our general direction. We're looking for the lands of she whose name cannot be mentioned."

"Yer headed for the lands of the evil queen?" Wayland's surprise was obvious. "I never heard nothin' good come outa' that place. 'Course, I never been there, neither. Yeah. I heeard that place is way east a' here."

"We want to find it so we can end Never Ever Land," the mole explained.

"Nobody can end Never Ever Land," Wayland sounded sure. "Never Ever Land is the end. Once yer here, yer here ta' stay. Beth sees ta' that. She owns the mirror."

"She owns a mirror?" Aleister quoted him in question.

"Yeah," the farmer nodded his head. "That's how I got here, my missus too. We met in Never Ever Land. We're raisin' our children here on this farm. It's a good farm and a good life, but what we both wanted was to be published."

"I think everyone in Never Ever Land got here from wanting to be published," the mole reminded himself. "You're lucky you weren't changed into anything."

"Whata' you mean, not changed inta' nothin'?" Wayland argued. "Look at me. I'm a Black and White. My missus is a White and Black. The kids are all mixed up. Some of 'em are Black and Whites and some of 'em are White and Blacks. We're right on the edge of Black and White Land. I suppose I should tell you about the rules here. "

"Rules?" Aleister was disappointed but not surprised. "Is this like Box Land where everyone has to wear a box on his head?"

"No," Wayland continued. "But I heeard about Box Land and it's just about as crazy. We live on the edge of Black and White Land and you're gonna to have to pass right through it to be on your way, so you best listen up. The only reason we ain't completely changed is because we live right on the edge and we can see that everything ain't black and white. We can see other people on the road beyond the creek and we can see they ain't Black and White or White and Black like us. But when you go farther into Black and White Land, you're gonna find people who are completely indoctrinated. They won't admit there is any color other than black and white. If you allow there's any other color they'll hang you."

"There's a death penalty for not being colorblind?" asked Aleister in disbelief.

"That's right," Wayland warned. "If you say the name of any other color than black and white in Black and White Land, you will be sentenced to death by hanging, so, when you go through there make sure you play a convincing act of being colorblind. You can't even see gray in that place and survive."

Walking under some trees along the side of one of Wayland's fields, the mole stopped, looked up into one of the trees. Pointing he asked, "Whaaaat is that, Wayland?"

The other two stopped and looked up. Aleister saw a large lizard with a big toothy grin, stretched out on the limb of the tree above them. "Lizards don't have teeth. What can that be?"

"Well, I wouldn't say that," the lizard startled them by answering. "Alligators have teeth. Caymans have teeth. Crocodiles have teeth. They're lizards. I'm a Cheshire iguana. We have teeth, but we only use them for grinning. Oh yes, Komodo dragons have teeth too. Big time."

"My, oh my," the mole softly commented. "It's a lizard that talks."

"I heard it too," Aleister looked up and saw the lizard. "Where did you come from?"

"Oh that's Celery, the Cheshire politician," Wayland continued walking. "When she grins, all you can see is her grin. She wants to be president of the United States, but here she is in Never Ever Land. She got here by trying to write books about how great she is, but she can't get past stealing the goodies from the White House, White Water and the Cattle Futures Scandal that was squelched just in time. That's not even mentioning the Foster affair. Even if she got elected, she'd never really be president because she's just a lizard."

"Well, at least she has a good head," the mole snickered.

"She needs a good head to be in the position she's in," Wayland agreed.

"She's a beautiful green," Aleister glanced back over his shoulder as they continued toward Wayland's home.

"Naah," the mole disagreed. "She's the same color as the bush."

"No, no no," Wayland interjected immediately. "You are entering Black and White Land. She's black. If you say, 'green' just a mile down the road, you'll be sentenced to death.' You gotta remember this is Black and White Land. There is no red, no green, no blue."

"Then what color is the sky?" Aleister tested him.

"It's white," said Wayland with certainty.

"I have a very good chance for election," the lizard called after them. "Watch this. When I'm talking to Black and Whites I can do this."

They watched as her dorsal ridge and grin turned black while the rest of her turned white. "And when I'm talking to the White and Blacks, I can do this." They continued to watch as her dorsal ridge and grin turned white, while the rest of her turned black."

"Politicians are all chameleons," Wayland snorted in disgust. "I don't trust any of 'em."

"I'm not a chameleon," insisted the lizard. "I'm a Cheshire iguana."

"Let's move along," urged Aleister. "I'm still hungry and this kind man promised he would give us food."

The style of the Zimmerman home made a whole new statement in extemporaneous architecture. It had three stories, with serendipitous additions added like afterthoughts. Cubes stuck out here and there enclosing whimsically added rooms. Some of them actually mounted on each other, one half on top and half hanging out over the lawn below. Some cubes had white paint. Others were black. The roof, a Cotswold Cottage sort of thing included rounded corners and thatching made from grasses that were impossibly interwoven, black and white. In the rear of the dwelling stood a large, conventional, red barn. Next to the barn, a corral enclosed black and white cows. On the other side of the barn, a large chicken coop contained Leghorn chickens, all white, naturally. A couple of hundred feet away from the house, the barn concealed a large hog pen full of black and white hogs.

As Aleister took in the unusual scene, a woman burst out of the house crying "Wayland. Where you been? I been gettin' worried 'bout you." Then she saw Aleister and the mole. "My word. My word. Wayland, is that a mole? He can't come in the house, ya know." Wayland introduced her as Ingrid Astrid Yvette Zimmerman.

"Yeah. Hi Ingrid," Wayland greeted her.

Slightly shorter than Wayland, her build was just as square with a round plump face, full lips, big brown eyes and a babushka on her head. Her black and white plaid dress hung to mid-length. She wore no shoes and her feet had obviously been in the garden next to the house for a few hours before Wayland returned home with his new friends. "I just love feeling the dirt between my toes," she later remarked. But for now, she was eyeing the mole suspiciously. "Wayland. Where did you find that thing?"

She was just as Wayland described her, a direct opposite to him. "Opposites attract, you know," she quipped about it over dinner. Wayland blushed and winked as she spoke, that is, of course if one could say that a Black and White even could blush.

Dinner was standard fair, but 'bodacious,' one might add, considering they had bodacious corn on the cob and pulled pork with Wayland's own black and white barbecue sauce. The food all came from the farm. "So," mumbled Wayland through a mouthful of bodacious corn, "I warned you about everything in Black and White Land being black and white. They get pretty fanatical about it downtown. You gotta be real careful what you say. Aside from that, the society here is pretty conventional."

Aleister glanced at the mole, who glanced back at him with a sort of hidden snicker. "Tha's right," Ingrid snorted. "But you bein' outsiders may get tripped up, an' they'll try to trip you up."

"Just do your best to keep your mouths shut," Wayland warned them again, "an' you oughta be alright."

CȜ Ȍ

Crystal Gooseworthy, a diamond ring on the finger of Ronald Flaass, squirmed and writhed against her imprisonment. A ring, being a sort of fixed instrument, doesn't have much wiggle room. That she couldn't move much made her even more agitated, but she could still speak, and speak she did. She spoke in Flaass's most private moments when her voice announced her presence, embarrassing him. She interrupted conversations with his enormous wife and this too embarrassed him. When new writers came through the mirror, she kibitzed, and this enraged him.

Finally, Crystal broke the last straw. Flaass, in an intimate moment with his wife, pinched Gertrude's cheek. Crystal announced loudly, "Wow. Talk about being able to pinch an inch. She's a real porker, Flaass. Surely, even you could do better than this."

Gertrude flung him off of her like a light blanket. Flaass hit the floor with a thud as Gertrude demanded at the top of her accomplished and powerful voice, "Ronnie, get rid of that thing..." Flaass flinched with the roaring sound. As his body hit the floor and he experienced the shock of personal injury, he heard her finish the sentence "...before I stick your head through that ring!"

Flaass picked himself up off the floor, walked out of the room. He took off the ring and directly addressed Crystal for the first time since he put the ring on his finger. "You know, young lady, I could turn you into a lump of coal and use you to cook my next hamburger."

Crystal had learned a thing or two about Flaass's habits with regard to what he turned people into. He turned her into a diamond because her first name was Crystal. He turned a young man named Kerry Stinkley into a Kerrier Pigeon, a sort of a cross between a pigeon and a hawk.

He turned Bill Barkley into a Birch Bark Canoe. The first rule, Flaass seemed to follow required making the victim squirm, so if Bill wanted to be a Cherry Tree, that's the last thing Flaass would have done. Bill hated the water, so Flaass made him into a canoe.

"I'd rather be a lump of coal than a goose," Crystal announced. "I'd really hate being a goose; all those feathers; gawd. I'm afraid of flying. I hate birds, especially geese. They're so mean. The Romans used them as guards at the edges of some of their cities. They called them the Praetorian Guard."

"Curse you," Flaass snarled. He then turned Crystal into a goose, a black and white one — and she promptly flew away.

C8   80

Aleister and the mole left the Zimmerman's farm early in the morning, with full bellies. Aleister's freshly washed clothing felt great. The mole slept in the garden with the firm promise that he would not dig in the ground, make a burrow or eat any of the roots in any of their gardens or lawn. Leonard had been a mole long enough that he no longer felt comfortable with being in a bed. He wanted to feel the ground under him, even if he was on top of it.

The day was clear with a blue sky (or, er, white — whatever). The hilly road was unpaved. "Quite a family," remarked Aleister amicably.

"I'm just a bit surprised we haven't seen any Preditors for the last few days," the mole worried aloud. "I doubt they've forgotten about us. I bet they just think we're hiding out in Flaass Land, and don't know we're looking for the evil queen. They don't know where to look for us yet, and that's okay with me."

"Well," began Aleister, "you have more experience with fleeing the Preditors than I do, so I guess I'll have to rely on you for those kinds of cautions. Mrs. Flaass threatened to send flying monkeys after me. I've been watching for them too."

"Hey, wait for me," they heard a voice calling behind them.

Aleister and the mole both stopped and looked back. Running along the road toward them was Celery the Cheshire iguana.

"Do we want her with us?" The mole watched as she drew nearer.

"Only if she can keep her mouth shut," remarked Aleister loudly enough that Celery heard him.

"If I talk too much, I'll just flash you my extremely charming grin and make my eyes sparkle with personality. Watch this."

Aleister turned to look at her. The iguana's body vanished except for the broad, white, toothy grin and sparkling eyes. "If Slick Willy got elected because the southern ladies thought he was 'just sa' cute,' what'll the guys think of this? I got the Rhodesian guy beat hands down. And with Hollywood buying Sow Cranken a seat in Minnesota, we'll actually achieve a subversive majority in Congress."

"I don't think a Cheshire smile and sparkling eyes are enough," grimaced the mole.

"Why not?" snorted Celery. "No one's paying any attention to much else. That's why what's-his-name called the voting public, 'sheeple.' With any luck at all, the country will be pure Animal Farm in no time. Bureaucracy rocks."

"Celery," Aleister warned flatly as he opened his penknife. "If you speak one more time, I'm going to have your tail for dinner."

The iguana hissed at him, turned off the path and scampered up a tree where she perched on a limb and displayed the white toothed grin once more. "What color am I now, white boy?"

"You're green," stated Aleister.

"Don't forget you're now in Black and White Land. If you don't bend to the popular creed, maybe I'll be having *your* tail for dinner." With that, she vanished completely.

Aleister and the mole could see a populated area with homes and businesses coming into view. All the people they saw were colored like Wayland and his family, Black and White or White and Black. The homes were painted all colors with equally beautiful landscaping. Most homes had flowers growing in front in window boxes or planters. Many of them had elaborate flower gardens in front or to the sides of the dwelling. One house ahead of them to the right had a trellis covered by a beautiful green vine blossoming in trumpeting purple flowers. "This is really a nice area," Aleister had to comment. "I've never seen that kind of flower before."

"They're Black Trumpets," a voice from nearby informed them. "They bloom all year long."

The voice came from a young girl, maybe eleven years old. Her white left side and her black right made her a White and Black. She had big blue eyes and in her white and black hair, she had a pink ribbon. She was wearing in-line skates and she seemed somehow fascinated with the giant mole and with Aleister's appearance. He was neither a Black and White nor a White and Black. "I've never before seen anyone who was all black or all white. There might be some people here who are a little bit afraid of you, but I'm not. My mom and dad talk about the all-whites and the all-blacks. They might think you're spies or something."

"We aren't spies," the mole hurriedly assured her. "We're just passing through."

"Where did you come from?" the little girl wanted to know.

"New York, actually. Ronald Flaass trapped us in Never Ever Land, over in Flaass Land. Flaass changed my friend Leonard here into a mole. He's not really a mole."

"He looks like a mole to me," she quipped suspiciously.

The girl skated along side them as they approached an intersection with a stoplight. The lights were red and green, just like in New York. Aleister, the girl and the mole waited till the light turned green to cross. A policeman stood watching on the corner as they stepped into the street. Just then, an automobile came screeching around a corner half a block away. When it approached the red light, it didn't even slow down. Aleister saw it just in time to pull the little girl out of its path. All three of them escaped unharmed. Aleister turned toward the policeman and said, "Didn't you see that? That guy ran a red light and nearly ran us over."

The little girl's eyes popped wide open. The mole placed both paws over its mouth. Together, they began edging away from him, trying to make themselves invisible to the policeman. Only then did Aleister realize what he had done. "Come here," ordered the policeman sternly.

He was a Black and White; white on the right. He wore and all black uniform except for the shiny badge on his chest. His tan pith helmet, much wider than his head permitted ventilation through tiny holes above the brim and bore the words "Color Police," on its front. He had a big gun in a holster by his side. He now drew his gun. "I ain't a traffic cop, sonny," he announced. "I'm a Color Cop, and you are under arrest for Chromopolyism. We call people like you 'Gray,' around here." He sneered when he articulated the word, 'gray.' "We don't put up with that disgusting life style. You'll surely be hanged in the morning. Come with me.

"The jail's this way. You walk in front and be careful of those bureaucratic cracks in the pavement. A man could fall into them, they're so big."

Aleister looked ahead to see what the cop was talking about. A concrete sidewalk stretched out ahead of him. In the distance he could see a big brick building with the word "Jail" in huge letters on its front and sides. Since they approached the building from one side, he could see behind the building, and what he saw caused him to shudder. There stood a large gallows, big enough to hang six men at once. Underneath it, a large dumpster yawned open, waiting.

The first Bureaucratic crack in the pavement was narrow and easy to hop over. The policeman followed, his pistol drawn and pointed at him. The next crack was bigger. Aleister thought he might need a running start to clear it. When he started to pick up his pace to jump the crack, the policeman ordered, "Hold it right there, boy. Where do you think you're runnin' off to?"

Aleister failed to clear this one because the policeman wouldn't permit him his running start. Down he fell. He had not realized the cracks were so deep in this bureaucracy.

Chapter 6: Aleister Becomes a Chicken Hauler

Aleister found himself sliding down a long chute. The moist, dirt chute smothered his freshly laundered clothes with thick, brown mud. The poor lighting revealed roots sticking out — reaching for him — and wriggling worm ends in the sides of the tunnel. The trip seemed endless, although it really passed quickly and ended in only a few seconds. The tunnel deposited Aleister in a shallow but swiftly flowing stream. *Well, now I'm soaked to the skin, but at least the mud will rinse out of my pants.* For the first time in days, Aleister thought of his latex gloves. It had been years since he had left his apartment with his hands bare. It surprised him that no debilitating illness had yet overtaken him.

After he finished rinsing the mud from his clothes and hair, he noticed a road above the stream. The occasional bicyclist rode by and every so often, a big truck roared past. He seated himself beside the stream on a large rock in the sunlight. As he waited for his clothes to dry, he started feeling sorry for himself. *What a predicament! I've been taking these nasty little jobs, like the one with Flaass, to keep body and soul together while I write, with hope against hope that someday, someone will recognize that my books are worthwhile and sellable.* He felt his face flush with anger as he reviewed his experience in Flaass's office. There, his job sickened him — rejecting manuscript after unread manuscript, setting up the reading fees for deposit and staying away from the mirror, paid by the minute, no less. *What a scam these spooks have going for them. They don't even take the time to sign or date their rejection letters. They just scoop off the reading fee and return the material — or sell it to be made into toilet paper.* His eyes smoldered again as he remembered the agent who sent him the rejection letter in his return envelope bearing six dollars worth of postage, with the note that the agent couldn't find the return postage to include the manuscript. *He threw away my manuscript and was too almighty stupid to see that the envelope he sent his unsigned letter in had six dollars worth of postage.*

The hopelessness and futility of the situation was overwhelming. He gazed longingly at the swiftly moving water. Disgust moved in quickly. The water wasn't deep enough for him to throw himself into it and drown. Another truck roared past on the road above. It had the words, "Feather and Hen Trucking." Underneath the slogan in smaller print, it advertised: "Chicken Haulers and Cluck Drivers wanted. Apply in person," but the first thought that came to mind had him wondering if being run over by a big truck would hurt much. *With my luck, I'd just be maimed for life. It might not kill me outright. I wonder if truck driving is a good job?*

He climbed the embankment to the road level. The two-lane road had a double yellow line down the center. He looked up and down the road for another truck when his eye fell on a sign announcing, "Dull Drome, 1 mile." He began walking.

The mostly level mountain road wound through the valley beside the creek. Trees hung over the road, with plants of all kinds creeping over the edge of the pavement. Wildflowers sprouted here and there. Squirrels ranged overhead in the trees. Aleister spotted the occasional red bellied wood pecker and a few brown thrashers. Other species appeared here and there. He even saw a rufus tohee. The wildlife held his interest till he came to the edge of the town. The sign outside labeled the village, "Welcome to Dull Dromes, Bethland, Never Ever Land." Beyond the sign, houses and shops lined the street. They were neither affluent homes nor poor ones. Some needed painting. Others missed a shingle or two from their roofs. Many front porches had bicycles on them and sparse porch furniture. Some of the homes sat on concrete blocks with crawl spaces beneath. Clotheslines and the occasional outbuildings, either garages or small storage sheds adorned the yards. Two convenience stores both offered gasoline and diesel fuel, a couple of blocks apart. The main feature of the town catching Aleister's eye, a huge truck terminal, appeared on the road rising toward the east beyond the village itself.

Row after row of fifty-three foot trailers stretched farther than Aleister could see behind a large office building. Beyond the offices another building contained a long row of truck garage bays. At the entrance, Aleister saw a turn style where a long line of trucks waited their turns coming into the terminal and leaving it. The red and white tractors pulling those trailers bore lettering on their sides saying "Feather and Hen Trucking." An added slogan stated simply, "We haul 'em. You choke 'em."

Everywhere Aleister looked, he could see 'wanted' posters hanging on telephone poles and trees advertising truck driving jobs with Feather and Hen. *Why not?* thought Aleister. *I don't have the courage to kill myself. I'm never going to find a publisher. I can't even teach. Every time I apply for jobs teaching English, I find there are two thousand to three thousand other applicants, most of them family members of the school board. Truck driving can't be that bad.*

Aleister spent weeks in Dull Drome, learning to drive those big trucks. Finally, they turned him loose with a load assignment and twenty five tons of live chickens in tiny cages. "Be in West End by tomorrow night," they told him. "That's fourteen hundred miles."

Aleister climbed up into the big cab, pushed the clutch to the floor and started the engine. The air pressure was already up to a hundred twenty pounds, so he put his foot on the service brake and released the trailer's spring brakes with a big "psssshhhh." Then he released the tractor brakes with another big "pssshhh." He dropped the range selector into low, ground the gear shift into third position and let the clutch out very gently. Ten miles down the road he saw a hitchhiker, way up ahead. As he drew closer, he discovered the hitchhiker to be a giant mole. Aleister began slowing the big truck, gearing down. By the time he was beside the mole, he eased it off the road and set the brakes. "Way'a y'all bee'in boy?" he inquired of the mole.

"Why are you talking like that?" protested the mole as he climbed in beside Aleister.

"Y'all know if ya gonna walk the walk, ya gotta talk the talk. Right?"

"Give me a break," complained the mole. "You're still Aleister Smiley aren't you? *Sprechen Sie Englisch, por favor.* Do you still have your thumb disc or have you completely dropped the idea of ever again putting pen to paper?"

"Yeah. It's here," Aleister fingered the object hanging on the lanyard around his neck. "But I have no hope of ever seeing any of it in print, unless I print it out myself."

"Chin up, man. Just because we're in Never Ever Land doesn't mean we'll always be in Never Ever Land. You could look at it like this: at least you're not a mole, a turtle or an iguana."

"Well, you've got a point there," admitted Aleister. "But you remember what Mrs. Flaass said, 'no one ever leaves Never Ever Land.' "

"Never is a long time, pal," reiterated the mole. "I seem to remember that we were on a quest, by the way. We were going to put an end to Never Ever Land by arranging for the demise of the Evil Queen."

"Oh yeah," Aleister remembered. "You-know-who, they say, lives somewhere to the east. Well, my truck's goin' west, right now and if I follow through on my first assignment, by tomorrow night, I'll be fourteen hundred miles west of here."

"That's a long truckin' trip for a lone chicken hauler," quipped the mole.

"Yes." Aleister ground the gear shift into third position again to pull out. "But at least I ain't a chicken choker."

"How do you feel about keeping all those birds cooped up in those tiny cages, anyway?"

"The cages are small, I guess," Aleister conceded. "They can't even stand up. They're exposed to the high winds from the speed of the truck and they have no shelter from rain, cold or anything else."

"Pretty cruel, if you ask me," charged the mole.

Aleister slapped both hands onto the steering wheel. He lowered his head, gritted his teeth and gave the mole a side-long look. "Exactly what do you propose I do? This is a good job."

"But it's part of Never Ever Land. If we don't finish the quest, we can never go home. We'll never be published, and worst of all, I'll always be a mole. Let's release the chickens and get out of here."

"Release the chickens?" Aleister repeated in shocked disbelief that he had heard such an outrageous idea. "Okay."

The cage doors turned out to be easy to open. Soon the air was full of white feathers. The chickens probably lived in those cages all their lives, dreaming, hope against hope for release. Without exception, they took to the wing and headed for the hills, just visible in the distance. One of the chickens, as it flew away sported a flashing green arrow on its behind. "Look at that," cried Aleister. "Did you see that?"

"See what?" The mole glanced up at the departing chickens.

"The flashing green arrow on the butt of that chicken. I can still see it, but it's getting pretty far away."

"That must be the right direction," speculated the mole. "Which way did it go?"

"East." Aleister pointed at the quickly disappearing chickens in the distance.

As they walked away toward the east, they chatted amicably, catching up. "How did you get away from that Color Cop, anyway?" The mole wanted to know. I thought you'd be swinging in the wind. I got out of there as fast as I could."

"I fell through the cracks," Aleister smiled. "Bureaucracy's best quality is its inefficiency. Its worst quality is the power to impose inefficiency on others."

Chapter 7: Glimmerland

The road Aleister traveled took him northwest, so when he and the mole headed east, they moved cross-country and off the road, toward the distant hills where the chickens had flown. None of them remained in sight. Most of the cultivated fields lacked easy passage, but Aleister and the mole were able to find a path leading east. They didn't have to trample any farmer's crops. They laughed about how eagerly the chickens flew the coop, so to speak. A thinly scattered trail of feathers led the way, but not one chicken could be seen anywhere.

The path to the distant hills stretched into the distance, gradually rising, an uphill climb all the way. As they hiked, the land became more natural until they found themselves surrounded in deep forest. "What's that light I've been seeing?" Aleister pointed to the sky in the east. "Have you been seeing it too?"

"Yep." The mole sounded breathless from the rapid hiking. "I was beginning to think it was my imagination. It seems to be coming from the sky beyond the crest of this hill."

They reached the top of the hill and began to descend. In the distance, they could see a large village with a park on the south side. The path they followed began to broaden, showing heavier use than it had on the way up the other side. "That flashing light in the sky is getting brighter," observed the mole.

"Is that an aurora borealis?" wondered Aleister. "I've never had a chance to see the aurora borealis."

"I doubt it," the mole disagreed. "The aurora borealis is supposed to be in the northern sky and this is to the south. How could that be?"

After rounding a bend in the path, they came upon a dirt road going east and west. "I think I must have passed this in the truck," Aleister suggested. "I passed a dirt road to the right. The sign said it goes to Glimmerland. I actually considered taking it so I could get a glimmer, so to speak."

Ahead of them on the road, almost in response to Aleister's remark, there appeared a sign reading, "Welcome to Glimmerland, Bethland, Never Ever Land." In the fine print at the bottom of the sign it said, "Come and enjoy our all natural Aurora Borealis, The Old Spanglish Fort and Diamond Lil's Historic Fountain of Couth." In very fine print there was a line that read, "Help Wanted — Apply in Person."

"Well," Aleister's sarcasm was obvious. "It seems there's always a place in Never Ever Land for someone who wants to work."

"At fruitless jobs, maybe," snorted the mole. "Dead end jobs and no pay jobs. Just for fun, let's see what the work is."

The road wound down into the small city, through houses and buildings that appeared to be hundreds of years old. Signs everywhere plugged discount tickets to the Fountain of Couth and the fort. The fort itself stood four stories high, a stockade made of rock. In the mortar, Aleister and the mole could see all sorts of colorful pieces of glass. On closer inspection, they discovered the glass consisted of marbles and colorful soda bottles that had been used in the cement. Seashells were visible here and there, as though the sand came directly from the sea without sifting out the seashells. The entrance crossed over a drawbridge suspended by very heavy ropes. The drawbridge led over a moat filled with water fed from a stream nearby. The fort's turrets held numerous rifle slots. From the gun deck on top large cannons peaked over the walls.

"This is neat." The mole gazed up at the walls and cannons. "Let's go in a see what's there. I wonder how it got the name 'Spanglish?' "

As they crossed the drawbridge, a net fell from high above them, capturing the mole. The bottom of the net was strung with a draw cord and as soon as the net had completely covered the mole, the bottom closed and he was hoisted aloft, screaming in fear. Voices from above were calling to each other, "Yeah. We got 'em."

Another called out, "Lil's gonna love this one."

"Is that a giant mole?" Another wanted to know. "More of Flaass's work, I'll bet. Beth doesn't do that to her victims."

"Yeah. Right," grumbled yet another voice. "Look at me. I'm a baboon. Beth did this to me."

Aleister stood there in shocked dismay, not sure if he should continue into the fort, or run away. He began slowly backing off of the drawbridge. *Did he say, "Lil's gonna love this one?" Who's Lil? We saw a sign back there that mentioned Diamond Lil. Is that the Lil? What are they doing to Leonard? Maybe I should slip into the fort and try to find out, but if I do, they might take me too. I can't leave him here.*

At that moment, a small automobile rumbled across the drawbridge right in front of Aleister. Inside the rear window, he could see the mole frantically waving to him. Aleister watched as the car drove down the entrance ramp from the fort. When it arrived at the street, it turned right, then right again when it reached the sign saying "Fountain of Couth." Aleister walked quickly to the end of the driveway just in time to see the back end of the car disappearing into a driveway about half a mile away. Aleister hurriedly followed. When he reached the driveway, he found himself standing underneath another very large sign repeating what the other one had said, "The Fountain of Couth," and "Entrance."

Aleister's greeting on entering the driveway was more crass commercialism. Signs everywhere bombarded him with information about 'couthness,' and the sights in the Fountain of Couth grounds. At the very entrance to the park was a smaller sign that promised, "Admission Free, if you leave here still Uncouth." Aleister walked in. Beyond the gate, a macadam pathway lined with elaborate landscaping partially concealed rows of cages. At that point, he heard a raucous sound overhead in the trees. He looked up and discovered the trees were crowded with roosting chickens, all clucking and crowing loudly at him. He stopped to watch them in consternation. As he watched, one of them flew to a limb on a tree above him, low enough that he could hear it clearly. When Aleister had calmed enough to notice, he heard the chicken saying to him, "Hey Al! Hey Al!" When it had got his attention it continued, "Thanks for freeing us."

"I wondered where you chickens went," answered Aleister. "I hope I don't get into too much trouble for that. I'll never get another job driving a truck. I abandoned the truck on the side of the highway. I released the cargo. I don't know what in the world I was thinking."

"Al," began the chicken. "We aren't chickens. We're poets. This is what Big Beth does to poets who come to her. She captures us, changes us into chickens and sends us to market. If it weren't for you, we'd all be chicken McDuckets by now or chicken fingers at McDeeps."

"So Beth is even worse than Flaass," muttered Aleister.

"She sure is," clucked the chicken. "By the way, before I was a chicken, they called me Swillin' Dillon. You can call me Dillon for short. We think you have several friends here," continued the chicken. "The mole is up ahead. They're putting him into his cage as we speak."

Aleister started to move in the direction indicated by the chicken when he heard a familiar voice to his right. He looked into the cage beside him and saw the disembodied grin of the Cheshire iguana. "How'd they catch you, Celery?" asked Aleister.

"They didn't have to," Celery answered through her Cheshire grin. "I came in on my own. This is a wonderful place. We have government-supplied food and free health care. We never suffer the responsibility of having to defend ourselves, so being stripped of all weapons was a big bonus. Here, we are never burdened with having to make decisions for ourselves. The government does everything for us. We are never offended with people who successfully strive to better themselves, uneven private property ownership or even retirement woes. Here, when we get old, instead of suffering the indignities of infirmity, they simply put us to sleep. This is heaven."

"Well," Aleister shook his head, eyeing the walls of Celery's cage. "It looks to me like you have finally found the place where you belong. By 'government,' I suppose you mean your jailer, Diamond Lil?"

Celery now materialized. Instead of black and white, she was her own natural green. Her dorsal fin was standing straight up and the grin was a sparkling white. Her eyes gleamed with happiness. "Here," she added, "I don't give a rat's behind if the cattle even have a future."

"Did I hear my name mentioned just now?" a voice inquired from the left.

Aleister turned and found beside him a flamboyantly dressed woman grinning broadly in the sunlight. The glitter from her front teeth was so distracting, that Aleister barely noticed her ankle length gown. It was burgundy with ivory trim and its hems were gleaming with embedded diamonds. Her willowy figure and narrow waist were amplified by the flowing tresses and exaggerated, lacy shoulders. At her throat was a lavish, gold-fringed cameo. Matching earrings occasionally peeked from under her waving, champagne-blonde hair. A delicate tiara clung to her hair and her eyes sparkled as much as her teeth as she assessed what she saw in Aleister. Only then did he realize the glittering effect from her teeth came from several diamonds she had embedded there.

"I'm Diamond Lil," she introduced herself with a glittering smile and an abbreviated curtsey. "Are you here to apply for the job?" Her voice matched her appearance, rising melodiously on the word 'job.' Her eyebrows lifted in inquiry as her wide smile broadened, waiting for a reply.

If I work here, I won't have to figure out how to justify hanging out around the Fountain of Couth, trying to figure out how to free the mole. I wonder how many others here need rescuing. I don't know if I can do it, but I certainly owe it to them to try — if I only can. Celery seems happy enough. I guess I'll leave her here.

"What is the job, Ma'am?" responded Aleister a bit shyly.

"It's a wonderful job," Lil gestured so that her hands more or less matched the lilting of her voice, as she spoke. "It's direct sales. You look like you'd be good at that. I have high hopes that you'll accept the position."

"And, uh, what would I be selling?" Aleister probed a little, thinking of his other direct sales experiences; life insurance, roofing and siding, baby pictures, greetings cards, sweepers. *I never really did very well in direct sales. I can be a people person for a while, if I try hard enough, but I really don't enjoy it very much.*

"The easiest thing in the world." Lil practically whispered in his ear, eyebrows raised and her right arm over Aleister's shoulders. "Couth. Everyone wants Couthfulness. People come here from all over the known world for a cup of Couth. That's what I sell."

Being so close to Diamond Lil, Aleister could see a bed bug creeping back up underneath her wig from where it had crawled. Aleister shuddered almost visibly as he asked, "What does it pay?"

"It's a very generous ten percent commission. Look at the line of people gathered to get their orders filled." She gestured toward a long line of people stretching around a corner of one of the buildings and out of sight. "They buy it by the cup, by the quart, and for very special customers, we sell it in bulk." As she spoke, her voice rose like an evangelist's, building momentum toward some ethereal point of theology.

"I think I might enjoy that for a while." Aleister tried to conceal his real feelings of disdain for the whole place. "Before I start, I think I'll need to find a place to stay. Can I get back to you later today or tomorrow maybe?"

"No need to worry about that," Diamond Lil's conspiratorial tones were back and her arm was back over Aleister's shoulders. "We'll supply everything you need; health care, food, shelter. Think of it, big guy. You could earn a fortune here. Come let me show you your new apartment."

Aleister knew that he was still five feet seven inches tall and he resented the patronizing compliment of "big guy." He had already begun to distrust Diamond Lil, when he first heard her name, while the mole was being kidnapped.

The chickens, roosting in the trees, began clucking loudly again, almost in warning. Lil looked up at them and for the first time, Aleister could see the meanness in her lips as they drew a tight line across her face. "Where did all these chickens come from? They showed up here just yesterday and they won't leave. Just look. There are chicken droppings everywhere. You have to be careful where you're stepping and if you're not careful, some may even hit you as it drops. And the feathers are making a mess. My groundskeeper is getting behind on cutting the grass. All he's getting done is sweeping up feathers and chicken dung."

As they strolled toward the back of the project, Aleister noticed that one of the cages contained a goose that began honking wildly. He glanced at it as they passed it. He passed two more cages before finding the mole. Aleister made a mental note, where to find the mole when he came back.

The apartment consisted of one room with one window and one door. "This will be adequate," Aleister glanced around the building. One room. Just like home. But why is there a lock hasp on the outside of the door?"

"Oh, we used to use this as a utility shed," Lil answered. "I'll have that removed."

His job consisted of standing in a large ticket booth and passing out different sized containers for a fee. The customers then took the containers to the well and dipped out what they wanted. The bulk purchasers ran a hose directly into the well, to pump water into tanker trucks parked outside the complex. Aleister billed them by checking the volume indicator on the side of the pump.

The park closed at five o'clock. After that, Aleister received a nice dinner of fried chicken, boiled, mashed pumpkins and greens. There he met Augustus Vedder, Lil's husband. He showed Aleister his end of the operation. He had a shop in the very back of the complex where he had captured a number of the chickens. There he was painting their wings a light brown, their breasts and heads a bright blue. He followed that by gluing head-dresses on them to cover their chicken-combs and long feathers on their tails so that they looked vaguely like Peacocks. Aleister felt sick, wondering where the chicken came from that he had just eaten.

"Do you realize," began Augustus, "these chickens are absolute archeological proof that the 6.098 hectares that makes up the Fountain of Couth grounds is the first piece of land created on Earth. Glimmerland followed the Fountain of Couth Grounds and of course, the rest of Never Ever Land was created last."

When he got away from Augustus, he wandered toward the front gate, but he stopped when he saw two Preditors standing there in company with a man wearing a box on his head, dressed like a policeman. Next to the Boxhead was another policeman. This one wore a tan pith helmet with the words on the front, "Color Police." Since the park closed at five o'clock, they couldn't get in and they were waiting there for morning, making sure Aleister didn't get away. Coming up behind them were two more policemen in company with Ralph Perez, the man who acted as Aleister's dispatcher at the Feather and Hens Trucking Company.

I'm had, Aleister groaned. *How did they find me? How can I get out of here?* They had not seen him because of the setting sun's failing light. Darkness was falling. They were standing in the parking lot where adequate light from the sky allowed Aleister to see them from the shadows and not be seen.

Aleister slipped quietly back into the park grounds, into the shadows. As he walked despondently toward his one room apartment, he heard a voice whispering from the shadows. It was the mole. "Hey. Get me out of here."

"Of course," answered Aleister softly. "Did you know that Celery the iguana is here too, and she likes it?"

"She's nuts. Everyone knows that. Get me out of this cage. Now would be just fine."

"That truck load of chickens is here roosting in the trees. Have you seen them?"

"What of it?" demanded the mole, impatient with Aleister's dallying.

"They told me they're poets, changed into chickens by Beth Tomawda. They say she hates poets and she always changes them into chickens then sends them off to a fast foods processing plant."

While Aleister fiddled with the latch, trying to figure out how to undo it, the mole continued, "Crystal Gooseworthy is here too. Do you know her?"

"Yes," replied Aleister as the cage door popped open. "She's a good friend of mine, but we have more of a problem than that." Aleister told him who was waiting at the gate.

As soon as the mole was free, he led Aleister to Crystal's cage. "It certainly has taken you long enough. That woman..." Crystal's voice shook with anger. "She promised she's saving me for Christmas dinner. Hasn't had goose in years. Can you imagine?"

"Listen. Crystal. We have to get out of..." the mole began.

"Just one minute, if you please," interjected a lilting and familiar voice from the shadows. A brilliant spotlight suddenly pierced the darkness, revealing Aleister and the mole holding Crystal's cage door open. She was about half way through it.

"Aleister Smiley," Diamond Lil continued. "After all the kindness we showed you, how can you find it in your heart to treat us this way, freeing our exhibits? You're even freeing my Christmas dinner, and Christmas is only a few months away." Her icy voice shook with anger and Aleister noticed something else alarming that he could see revealed in the light she carried. The Box Head Policeman, the Color Cop, the preditors and the policemen with Aleister's former truck dispatcher all stood behind her in the shadows. She had let them in and led them to him.

"Ma'am," the Box Head Cop interrupted her. "Is there someplace where we can lock them all up, real handy like, till morning? I think me and the other boys here are pretty tired and we could use some sleep. We been chasin' these fellas all day."

"We'll lock them up in Aleister's apartment. That's why the lock hasp is still on the door," she muttered through clenched teeth. "We usually keep it locked during the night anyway."

A few minutes later, locked in Aleister's one-room shed, the three of them sat looking at each other in the dim light of a one bulb dangling from the ceiling.

"This is just great," moaned the mole. "Crystal and I are locked up in your apartment with you because YOU refused to put on a box hat, YOU released a truck loaded with chickens and YOU had to go and say 'red' in Black and White Land."

"Whadya mean ME," retorted Aleister. "Releasing the chickens was your idea. You also refused to screw a box to your head, and the light WAS red."

"Enough," the goose intervened. "We're in a bad enough situation without you two starting to fight."

"How did you wind up in Never Ever Land anyway?" Aleister demanded of Crystal.

"I had to come in here to find you two and I still haven't found my other friend, Jonathon Peach. He's got to be here somewhere. I wonder what Flaass changed him into."

"It doesn't look like we're ever going to find out," Aleister observed sarcastically. "Leonard and I are apparently going to jail. After jail, I'll be executed by the Black and Whiters and you'll be Christmas dinner for Diamond Lil and her husband."

CЗ   ВО

The Color Cop volunteered to guard Aleister's door for the night and keep the three of them locked up. He could hear them arguing inside, but he didn't pay much attention. The way things like this usually worked, Aleister and the mole would go to the other jurisdictions and pay for their crimes with prison time. Then Aleister would be extradited to Black and White Land and there executed in accordance with the law of the land.

CЗ   ВО

No padlock to use on Aleister's door hasp made both cops very un-happy. Diamond Lil said there'd be no need for such a thing. She pro-duced a nail and dropped it into the hasp's hole, very effectively elimi-nating the possibility that the latch could be undone from inside the building. "And with one of you sitting here all night, there is no way anyone else could come along and release them."

The Color Cop sat down on the top step of the three leading to Aleis-ter's door. It had been a long day. Before long, he moved to the short porch in front of the building and stretched out on the lounge chair. In a short time, he fell asleep. When his snoring reached a pitch al-most loud enough to be heard by those inside the cottage, three white chickens landed quietly on the ground in front of him. One of them crept around onto the porch and squatted right in front of the snoring policeman. A second one crept to the other side, placing the policeman between itself and the door. The third chicken, when the first two were in place, emitted a single cluck.

Out of the trees, several hundred more chickens quietly glided to the ground and in turn, hopped up the three steps to the porch level. They waddled quietly back and forth on the porch, dropping on the floor the things that chickens are prone to drop. When they were satisfied that the floor was adequately slippery, except for right in front of the door, of course, the chicken who had been waiting flew up to the door hasp and quietly removed the nail holding the latch in place. It dropped the nail in the grass beside the door and pulled the hasp open, releasing the door.

Aleister and the mole were asleep, but Crystal was not. They found her sitting in the middle of the floor, silently weeping when the door swung open. She sat there in astonishment as a chicken stepped through the door and whispered, "Hey, you guys. Let's go before that cop wakes up."

Aleister didn't hear the chicken, but the mole did. He rolled over, sat up and nudged Aleister who had been sleeping poorly. He started with a full voiced "What is it?"

"Quiet," whispered the chicken and Crystal together.

By then, Aleister had looked around and gathered a little bit of what had happened. The door stood open. No one was around but the chick-ens and the sleeping cop. Darkness shrouded the grounds and silence filled the night. "Let's get out of here," he whispered urgently.

Crystal stuck her head out of the door first. She could see the cop snoring on the lounge chair. She hopped out and glided silently to the ground, turned and waited for the other two. Next came the mole, who slid out quietly on his stomach down the three steps to the ground.

Aleister came last. As he stepped on the first step, it squeaked. Everyone froze and looked toward the cop. The cop stopped snoring, but didn't move.

They waited. In a few minutes, the cop changed positions on the lounge chair and another minute later he began snoring again. With his heart in his throat, Aleister moved his other foot to the second step. When he placed his weight on it, it did not squeak. He tried to move as slowly and quietly as he could, but while they were waiting for the cop to start snoring again, a gentle breeze picked up and unbeknownst to any of them, the door to the cottage began to swing quietly back and forth. Some of the chickens saw it and in some way quietly communicated it to the rest of the flock that by now numbered over five hundred chickens.

Aleister slowly and deliberately moved his foot off of the top step. It made no sound. He continued the motion of his foot to the bottom step and put his weight on it, keeping his foot to the side of the step hoping it would be less likely to squeak. He succeeded in getting his weight completely to the ground before the wind picked up a little more and the door slammed shut with a BANG. The cop woke up.

As he did, five hundred chickens flew at him, pecking and squawking, flapping their wings and making a general raucous uproar. One remaining chicken on the ground, pecked at Aleister's leg and urged him, "Follow me, quickly."

The three of them followed the chicken to an unlocked gate in the rear of the property. Outside the gate they found the stream that flowed past the Old Spanglish Fort. Pulled up on the bank a small rowboat waited, just big enough for the three of them. They piled into the boat in the darkness of the night, and pushed off, not making a sound.

Chapter 8: The Valley of the Shadow of Beth

The flow of the river carried them at a brisk pace, but the darkness prevented them from clearly seeing the occasional rocks looming out of the water ahead. The collision with the first one almost ejected Aleister from the boat. After that, they watched carefully, trying to see the rocks before striking them.

"There's another one," the goose warned frantically.

Aleister, the only one of the three with hands that could be used with the boat's oars sat in the center seat, a hand on each oar, trying to guide the boat. "Quickly, to the right," came Crystal's guidance. Aleister swung the boat to starboard and rowed hard.

"That's enough," the goose called out, watching intently for the next one.

"There's one coming up on the left," the mole fearfully cautioned. "But I think it's far enough away that's we'll miss it, if you can just lift the left oar high enough."

They floated past the next rock, but the oar grazed a plant growing out of the top of it, swinging the boat's nose to the left. Aleister quickly corrected. Overhead, Aleister could see the shadows of many birds on the wing. With some surprise, he realized those birds were their friends, the chickens. "That's really strange," Aleister observed softly. "Look at those chickens way up there in the sky. Chickens can't fly like that."

"But those are flying like that," Crystal reminded him. "Don't forget, they're not really chickens. They're poets. Poets can fly anywhere. That's what poetry is. It lifts the spirit so that the imagination soars."

If she hadn't been a goose, they would have noticed the dreamy look in her eye.

She's thinking of that poet, what's his name — oh yeah, Jonathon Peach, Aleister groaned inwardly. *I wonder what happened to him. He's obviously here in Never Ever Land somewhere. I wonder if we'll bump into him before we get away. I wonder if we'll ever get away.*

Not far ahead on the right bank, they could see the looming shadow of the old Spanglish Fort, Fort Carrion, towering overhead. Aleister could see figures moving on the gun deck, the top level of the fort. Antique cannons once used by the Spanglish poked out here and there, where they had once guarded the river from invaders and pirates. Aleister watched in rising panic as the shadows of many men pushed ramrods into the mouths of those iron behemoths. *I wonder why they're loading those cannons? I hope they aren't planning to shoot them at US.*

"What are they doing up there?" whispered Crystal.

"Shhh." The mole held one of its long claws to its lips. "Let's get past here as quickly as we can. It could be first light soon. If we can get out of range before they can see us, they won't be able to shoot at us."

"How far can they shoot those things?" Aleister could feel rising panic. "Does anyone know?"

The goose replied, "I heard someone talking about them while I was in that cage in the Fountain of Couth. They said the cannons could be fired with great accuracy for up to three point eight miles."

"If that's true," groaned the mole, "and we have about half a mile to go before we're even there, we have to go over four miles before first light, when they'll be able to see us."

Ever so quietly, they maneuvered the boat around the rocks. Aleister brought one of the oars aboard and used the other one as a paddle, making less noise but with less efficiency. He could see the shadows of the men moving around on the ramparts against the lighter background of the sky. The goose entered the water and used her swimming skills to help Aleister manipulate the boat. She stayed near the bow watching out for rocks and pushing the boat's nose in one direction or the other, while Aleister was in the stern providing locomotion. The mole hid on the bottom of the boat, trying to be invisible.

There was a tremendous flash of light. A moment later, they heard a canon's roar from the fort. They could see the smoke rising above it and drifting slowly downstream. A moment later, a large rock about a hundred yards behind them exploded in a huge splash of water. Cheers were coming from the gun deck on top of the fort, followed by less heartening sounds. Aleister could make out the words of someone shouting, "We hit a bleeding rock. It wasn't them at all. Where are those blighters at?"

Aleister could feel the fear rising in his throat. He could see them on the gun deck, reloading the canon. The goose took refuge on the side of the boat opposite the fort. The mole quivered in his hideout on the boat's bottom. Now abreast of the fort they could hear the voices more clearly. Aleister could feel one other thing, a new thing, and he could see a change in the surface of the water as it reflected the night sky. The current had begun moving faster. The surface ahead was exposed in the first light of morning. The sun would be up in another half an hour at the most. Soon, they would be plainly visible from the fort and an easy target if they didn't make some speed — soon.

Aleister dropped the oar he had used as a paddle back into the oar-lock. He unboarded the other oar and began rowing downstream as hard as he could. The goose swam around to the boat's stern and began pushing from behind. The mole continued to quiver on the floor of the boat. They had about three miles to go, racing the sun. Another flash burst from the fort. They could see the smoke again drifting down-stream from the fort's gun deck. A huge splash of water rose about a hundred feet behind them. Cries from the fort damned the clean miss.

Aleister rowed harder as the current picked up speed. He reckoned they were making about ten miles per hour between his rowing and the current of the stream. Aleister figured it would take about twenty-four minutes to get beyond the 3.8 mile range limit of the canons. How long would it be till they could be seen well enough for an accurate shot? Maybe ten to fifteen minutes at the most, he figured, but the stream bore away from the fort about half a mile ahead of them. Once they rounded the bend of the stream, the trees on the banks would conceal them. They'd be out of sight of the fort. How long till then?

Another flash burst loudly from the fort, followed by a second and a third, each followed by the cannon's roar. A huge splash fifty yards ahead of them marked the landing point of the first ball. The second whizzed past Aleister's nose, close enough that he could feel the wind from it. The ball made contact with a rock twenty-five yards to his left. The third struck the water about fifteen feet behind them, dousing the boat, drenching Aleister. Water now sloshed back and forth on the deck of the rowboat. Aleister began considering abandoning ship, when he heard screaming from the men on the gun deck of the Old Spanglish Fort.

The cannon fire stopped. Aleister looked behind them at the fort and saw a cloud of white swirling around the canons. The screams of the men on the gun deck brought the goose around to the fort side of the boat. The mole sat up. "What's going on?" he wanted to know.

"Look," Aleister pointed with his chin.

Crystal watched in amazement. Aleister's eyes were glued to the scene. The mole before turning his head to look, pointed out, "If you don't row, we're going to hit another rock."

Aleister quickly returned his attention to their situation on the river and corrected their course.

"I can't believe they're doing that." Crystal watched, wide-eyed.

"Neither can I," exclaimed the mole.

Aleister turned to watch again, as the cloud of chickens that had been flying high overhead attacked the men on the gun deck of the fort. All he could see were feathers flying. Occasionally a single bird would lift above the tangle and then disappear into it again.

"Aren't you glad, now, that we released them?" asked the mole. "They saved us at the Fountain of Couth and again now. For what? We released them. How long do they owe us?"

"If it weren't for us," Aleister reminded him, "they'd be chicken salad by now. I'd be grateful. Wouldn't you?"

ɞ ʚ

In the shadows slightly upstream from the fort, Ronald Flaass stood stock still, dressed in his blue rabbit suit, frowning deeply. Beside him stood his wife Gertrude, chewing her lip and muttering under her breath. Flaass watched the canons miss his quarry time after time. His fury grew and Gertrude was becoming restive. With them were three Preditors assigned to capture Aleister and bring him back to Flaass-land.

"We'll get him yet, sir," one of them assured him just now, interrupting Flaass's dark thoughts.

The attack of the chickens was a complete surprise to Flaass. As he watched with his brow darkened even more. The chickens dived and clucked, pecked and squawked and the cannon fire stopped. Flaass turned to his wife and said, "Alas, what miscreant has conceived this fowl dilemma?"

ɞ ʚ

The boat with Aleister, Crystal the goose and Leonard the mole drifted quietly into the sunlight, beyond the bend in the creek. The chickens were back overhead. The occasional splat of chicken guano struck the deck of the boat, always followed by Crystal's, "Eeeeoooh," and Aleister's plucking up of the muscle shell Crystal had found for him. With the muscle shell, he scooped the chicken guano out of the boat and dropped it in the river.

The boat drifted into deeper and deeper ravines with mountains towering overhead. The river entered a light rapids for while, while the three sat in the boat shuddering about what might lie ahead. The chickens flew nonchalantly, some far ahead. Aleister felt, if there was danger, their eyes in the sky would alert them, but now it was Crystal saying, "But they're just chickens. How would they know if we're in danger?"

"What do you mean, 'just chickens?'" retorted Aleister with a chuckle. "I thought they were poets whose words lifted the spirit to soar? And look what they just did for us at the fort!"

"It's 'imaginations' lift their spirits. You don't listen very well do you?" blurted the goose.

"No need to start bickering," interjected the mole. "We're now entering the Valley of the Shadow of Beth. See the sign over there? This could be even more interesting than Glimmerland. Just look at that," he added pointing.

Along the river bank to their right a small park surrounded a looping, drive-around roadway. The nicely landscaped park contained small bushes beside the loop with trees in the grassy area between. Large, pleasingly rounded river rocks marked the bends in the loop. Beyond the park area, a road paralleled the river and beyond that, the mountain rose in a shear cliff with exposed rocks, and trickling water from concealed springs.

A long snakelike vehicle drew their attention. It was composed of five carts, covered on top to keep out the rain and open on the sides so the wind could blow through easily. A small tractor at the head of the train was designed to look like an old time steamboat. The driver's attire resembled that of an old time railroad conductor with a flat topped, billed hat and with a badge on the front. He wore a vest with a watch chain and a whistle on a lanyard around his neck. A metal bracket fixed around his head supported a microphone held close to his mouth and he talked rapidly over a public address system connected to the five carts.

Morbidly obese people crowded the carts, all talking loudly. Many of them carried fishing equipment. Their beefy hands dwarfed the thin fishing poles. Many of them trailed a string of equally blubbery children. Numerous people slouched along the edge of the river soaking bait, while others engaged in the exercise of either boarding or exiting the vehicles, some so heavy they could barely walk. To get from the vehicle to the river, they swayed from foot to foot. On each sway, they would move one of their feet forward a few inches, then swing their enormous weight off the other foot to the one they had moved forward. In this way, they gradually worked their way to the stream or back to the tram. Some excitement now drew Aleister's attention. One of the people had become jammed between the handholds of the cart she was riding. Several others tried to help her work her girth through the handholds so she could go fishing. Since those helping nearly equaled the size of the trapped person, the work produced a serenade of grunting and good-natured cussing. All of them sweated profusely, struggling to manage their own weight as well as trying to help the stuck woman get free.

The big lady finally made it through the handhold barricade with a slight popping sound. Finally free, she reached back into the vehicle and pulled out a cooler and picnic basket loaded with diet drinks and junk food. Before she reached for it, she took a bite from a big crispy looking, cream filled donut. With her mouth working on the new bite, she reached into the cart for her supplies. As she pulled her picnic basket off of the cart, they noticed, on top of the picnic basket, a big white bag labeled "McDeep's Deep Fried Delights." In the fine print under the label it said, "Super Size and Save."

"She's really big," the mole needlessly pointed out. "Those handholds that trapped her must be five feet apart."

"Whatever." Aleister chose to ignore the scene. "I think we should ditch this boat and move on. Those trains look like just the way to do it. I wonder if we have to pay to ride them."

Before they got their boat to the riverbank, the train pulled out. The people fishing watched with fanatic attention as Aleister and his party approached. Aleister could hear them talking as the boat drew nearer. "My goodness, Martha. Just look how emaciated that poor young man is. And what's that with him? He has his pet goose and good heavens ... is that a mole?"

"Why is he so skinny, Ma?" came the voice of a very round little boy. "Is that how people look from other places?"

"Don't forget, Porky. In the Valley of the Shadow of Beth, a man isn't growed up till his belly bounces off of his knees. Just look at your Daddy." The man struggled to his feet as he spoke, to demonstrate what he had just described. But as he got to his feet, his fishing pole started jumping and in his effort to land the fish that had struck his line, he fell into the stream. The others gathered around, each grabbing a hand, or his shirt. One threw him a rope and four people put their generous weight into pulling him back out of the water.

"My gawd, Dumphrey," scolded the very round woman seated on the ground next to where he had been sitting. "That was close. Try to be more careful."

Aleister and his friends learned that the trains arrived every fifteen minutes, so they didn't have long to wait. The local city government provided the ride, they were told, so they didn't have to pay anything. The vehicle bumped and pitched down the mountain road into the Valley of the Shadow of Beth. The conductor lectured, told stories and joked. Through his efforts and in spite of the loud conversations around them, they learned all about the valley's history, the corporate success of McDeep's and the wonderful, or terrible, power of Beth. Along the road's side, they could see signs and billboards with slogans and advertisements, all involving Beth Tomawda. One of them had a picture of a thick, hard bound book titled, *How to Lose Fifty Pounds in a Month; the Sensible Way*. Another advertised Beth's services as a literary agent and ghostwriter. The slogan underneath stated, "If anything can prevent you from becoming a writer, let it."

"Well, that's real positive," groaned the mole.

"It sort of lays it on the line," observed the goose. "She's just like Flaass. I bet all the books written here are generated by Beth's computer and signed by Beth herself. She must be another monster like Flaass, just bigger."

"I know you folks is new to this area," a deep voice mentioned conspiratorially from the seat behind them. "But you better learn real quick who's boss around here or you'll pay bitterly. Beth ain't no one to fool with. One thing you should know right up front. Beth don't like no skinny people. You better stay out of her sight. Here, when Beth eats, we all eat. Why do you think we're all so big? She owns McDeeps. And we all work at McDeeps, so we have to eat there."

On the last stretch, down a steep and rocky incline, Aleister could see a valley completely in shadows. It puzzled him because the sun was shining brightly overhead. It wasn't till they rounded the last turn into the village that he could see an enormous statue erected on the hillside above the town. It was the image of a large woman. Her eyes were bright, as though they were lighted from behind. Wavy and long hair framed full, pink cheeks. Her lips appeared to be busy chewing something and her ample girth blocked the sunlight coming from above. In front of her enormous stomach she wore a white apron bearing the slogan, "McDeep's Deep Fried Delights," followed by "Supersize and Save." Finally, Aleister understood why the place was called, "The Valley of the Shadow of Beth." The entire valley was beneath her shadow. It was only then that he became aware of a McDeep's fast food restaurant on every single corner of the village.

The train began to slow because it was entering the village. With alarm, Aleister spotted a small crowd gathered near the town square, not far ahead of them. Among the people gathered there stood an extremely large woman who looked just like the statue on top of the hillside. Beside her stood a tall figure dressed in a blue rabbit suit. Beside him stood a woman who was most certainly Gertrude Flaass. With them were three Preditors, the Boxhead policeman and the Color Cop. Aleister looked up at the sky; no chickens. He could feel gloom overwhelming the scene, gloom that could be felt everywhere the Preditors appeared. As soon as Crystal spotted them, she took to flight and disappeared over a distant hill to the east of the Valley. The mole began quivering. Aleister froze to his seat.

As the train pulled to a stop in front of the small gathering, he could hear Flaass's voice announcing, "He's mine at last."

"Oh no he's not," boomed the deep alto voice of Beth. "He's mine."

"Excuse me," interjected the Color Cop. "He's really mine. He has a rendezvous with fate back in Black and White Land. I must take him with me."

"You can't have him till we're through with him," announced the Boxhead Cop. "After he gets his box, you can take him back to Black and White Land and do whatever you want to with him."

"Just where," boomed Beth, "do you fools think you are?"

At the word "fools," Flaass's eyes flared. He drew a deep breath while Gertrude tugged on his arm, trying to get his attention so he would keep his mouth shut. He raised his hand and pointed his index finger at Beth. Shaking it in anger, he shouted, "You fat floozy! Who do you think you are to try to deny me ... me ... Ronald M. Flaass my prize? I tracked this miscreant from..."

That was as far as Flaass got. With the snap of her fingers, Beth turned him into a real blue rabbit that went slowly hopping across the grass, nibbling here and there on the occasional clover he found there.

Mrs. Flaass's eyes went wide in shock. The Color Cop and the Boxhead both stepped back a few steps. The Preditors took to wing and disappeared in the direction of the west, toward Flaassland. Gertrude sputtered a few times before she found her voice. By this time, Beth had turned to her and was scowling deeply, her lips still moving as though she were chewing something. As that thought registered on Aleister, he noticed her bring her hand to her mouth and she took a bite of a large piece of fudge. Mrs. Flaass gained control of herself and she stopped sputtering. She charged Beth and began slapping and punching her ample cheeks. Beth's plump cheeks rolled back and forth in little waves with the force of Gertrudes blows. Pieces of fudge flew from Beth's mouth as her head snapped back and forth under those beefy fists. Aleister and the mole slipped off of the train on the side opposite the scene taking place between Beth and Gertrude. A gathering crowd of astonished fat people gave Aleister and the mole plenty of cover where they could disappear and make themselves invisible while they slipped away toward the east and the land of the one whose name cannot be mentioned.

Chapter 9: Print on Demand Land

Slipping out of the Valley of the Shadow of Beth, Aleister and the mole stayed off the road. They kept to the shadows of the trees and the forest. They didn't stop till they were completely out of the valley, on top of the next mountain and starting down the other side. Aleister couldn't resist dropping into a McDeeps and getting a bag full of hamburgers on the way out of town, so he did have food available, although he objected to the grease he ingested with every bite.

"Just what are we doing?" he demanded of the mole as they rested under a large oak tree. "We're having misadventure after misadventure."

"We established two goals when we first met," said the mole. "We want to find the evil queen so we can end Never Ever Land. And we want to get out of Never Ever Land. I guess those both sound like they're the same goal. If we ever do find the evil queen, we have no idea what to do to stop her, to, you know, end the existence of this awful place."

"No," said Aleister. "We may have to take her life. I never killed anyone before and I'm not sure I want to, even if she is pure evil. You know, it may be as simple as dumping a bucket of water on her, like Dorothy did in *The Wizard of Oz*. The old witch just dissolved. But Karma seems to take care of those who need it. We'll just have to sort of, play it by ear."

"Karma shmarma," said the mole. "If we don't take care of it, it won't get taken care of. Maybe there's some token she has that gives her so much power. We can destroy it. We have plenty of help."

"I haven't seen the chickens today," said Aleister. "Well, not since this morning. I don't know where they went. And speaking of reinforcements, where has Crystal gone? She fled like the morning dew as soon as she saw Flaas. It looks to me like it's just the two of us again."

"I would have disappeared too if I could have," said the mole. "In fact, we both did as soon as we could."

The forest was growing thicker as they continued their walk. They eventually had to slow down, picking their way around bushes and thick undergrowth. "I don't see why we don't just go back to the road, if we can find it," Aleister grumbled.

"Not a good idea," they heard a voice state from over their heads. "But if you head off to your right a little bit, you'll find a path that will be easier to use than just marching through the woods, like you have been doing."

Aleister and the mole both looked up. A chicken had landed on a tree above them. "You two certainly made yourselves hard to find. If we couldn't find you, Flass certainly won't. But we did find you. At least I did. Now I have to go and tell the others where you are. I'll be back. Please don't wander far." With that, the chicken flew off above the trees. High in the sky, they could hear the classic chicken sounds of, "Aaaak Baaaak." In time, it faded off into the distance.

Aleister and the mole found the path mentioned by the chicken to be going in the right direction, east. It descended the mountain toward another valley where they could see large office buildings in the distance. The path eventually met with another road appearing to lead directly into the valley. At the edge of the community was a sign that said, "Print on Demand Land." Underneath the slogan was a statement: "For instant publication of your special novel, come to 115 Maine Street and see Carleen Alder."

"Well," said Aleister. "That looks hopeful. What do you think?"

"Don't forget we're in Never Ever Land," answered the mole. "Never Ever Land means you'll Never Ever get published if anyone here can help it."

"Still, it might be worth a shot."

Carleen was a woman to Aleister's liking. She was five feet seven inches tall, the same as Aleister, and ageless. She had a ready and wide smile, which she gleamed on Aleister as he walked through her door. Her hair was neck length, gray and streaked with red. Her make up kit was lying open on her desk and it included the pallet knife she obviously used to apply it. The thick makeup covered the deep crevasses the years had imposed upon what must have once been a very charming face. Her voice was cheerful and when she saw Aleister appear at her door, her face lit up in happiness.

"I'm so glad to see you, young man. I'm Carleen Alder. What's your name?"

After the preliminaries and small talk, Aleister announced that he wanted to submit a book for publication. Carleen's eyes lit up even brighter than they had when Aleister walked through her door. "You've certainly come to the right place," she said. "Here's our contract." She pulled out a sheaf of papers from a desk drawer and slid them across the desk to Aleister.

As Aleister read the contract, passing each page to the mole as he finished, his face grew dour. "Let me see if I understand this right," Aleister said. "You are going to charge me $50,000 up front. For that money, you will set up the book to be printed on demand, that is to say, if and when you sell one, you will print one. You will not publish any copies to be distributed to bookstores. You will not advertise the book. You will not contact any potential sources that may result in a screen play. The only marketing or advertising for the book will be handled by me personally through my web page, once I get a web page. If I buy a book, I get a thirty percent discount, but to get the discount I have to buy one hundred books at the retail price of $20.00. All sales of my book that you achieve through your web page will pay me a royalty of one dollar and twenty-five cents. Am I getting it right, so far?"

"What a deal," squealed Carleen. "And once we sell ten thousand of your books, we will expect another $50,000 to guarantee the printing of ten thousand more."

"Let's see," said Aleister. "If you sell the first ten thousand books, at a royalty of one dollar and twenty-five cents each, I would make $12,500, less the cost of my advertising and promotion. If I sell all ten thousand myself with the thirty percent discount, I would gross $60,000, less the cost of the marketing, mailing, and storage."

"It doesn't sound like much profit," said Carleen, "but just think of it. You're book will actually be in print. You'll be a real author."

"Wow," said Aleister, rolling his eyes. "And you haven't even checked out my manuscript."

"If you don't have the money in your pocket," giggled Carleen, "and most of our clients don't, there is an ATM machine on the corner. You can get the money there."

"I think maybe we'll go and check into that. Thanks so much for your time."

"Don't forget," called Carleen, as they walked out the door. "There are lots of print on demand publishers here in Print on Demand Land, but none of them print as good a quality work as we do. We bought state of the art equipment when we opened this business, in 1980. Ours is the best."

Aleister was feeling discouraged. The mole remained silent. The next shop they came to had a sign on the front that said, "Johannes Gutenberg Press, Print on Demand." They looked in the windows and saw a man there, wearing an apron, working on a large wooden vice. He would insert a frame loaded with one page of a book using hand carved, wooden letters, into the vice, then tighten it using large cranks at either side of the vice. A sign on the counter in front of the store said, "sign up now to have your book published. Ten copies only, ready in six years. Cash in advance. $26.87 per page, per copy."

They retreated to a small central park across the street where they ate the last of the McDeep hamburgers. There was a river running through the town. Across the street beyond the park, Aleister saw sea birds circling. He told the mole, "I'm going to go have a look at the river. I think that may be the same one we floated down a few days ago."

As he strolled across the street, his thoughts were turning dark. *My books are never going to have a chance. Every time I think there's an opportunity, it turns out to be another rip-off like with Flaas. Print on demand is another scam. It's great if all I want is to give away a few copies to family and friends, but to actually mass market the book, it's not practical. I suppose a few writers have made it that way, but if my book isn't good enough to stand on its own feet, then I think it shouldn't stand at all. My books just aren't good enough to get past the editors, or preditors as the mole calls them. Maybe I should just jump in this river and drown.*

He glanced back into the park where the mole was sitting. *Poor Leonard. He can't get published either. There are so many of us caught here in Never Ever Land. It's so hopeless, so futile. To make matters worse, there is such a large industry focused on stripping anyone with any hope of all the money they have in return for what — a book on the mantel piece? I wish I had a mantel to put one on.* He began eyeing the river again, wondering what drowning would be like.

A goose floating in the water below him suddenly took flight, climbed out of the river basin and landed at his feet. "Aleister," Crystal said to him, "you look really low. You okay?"

"I'm just feeling a bit discouraged by all this," said Aleister. "Here we are in Never Ever Land. None of us stand a chance at getting published here. This land is a prison of desperation and futility. None of us has any hope."

"Tsch Tsch," clucked the goose. "We so often use momentary feelings to determine our own worth. How did you feel about yourself while you were writing the book?"

"Exhilarated," said Aleister. "I lived in the world I was creating, for a while. When I was finished I was disappointed that it was over and I wanted to start another make believe world to live in. How do you feel when you write?"

"When we were in the Valley of Beth, I talked with one of the cooks at a McDeeps. He was feeling pretty bad about himself too. He must have weighed over four hundred pounds and he was feeling bad about his job and his body. You know what he said to me? He said, 'I am not my job. I am not my body.' Neither are you, Aleister. Neither is Leonard. Neither am I. We're going to get out of Never Ever Land. Just you wait and see."

They could hear a commotion behind them. They turned to look back into the park and to their horror, they saw Flaas standing there. He was no longer a blue rabbit. Now he was dressed in a tuxedo, top hat and bow tie. A large horse stood at his side, strangely wearing the same skirt and sort of a matching top they had last seen Gertrude Flaas wearing. The mole was surrounded. Aleister and the goose stepped behind a tree.

"There's nothing we can do to help him," Crystal whispered desperately. "Where are the chickens? Do you think they can do something?"

"Look behind Flaas. On the ground," whispered Aleister. "Is that a blue rabbit?"

"It is," whispered Crystal. "Then what's with the guy in the tux? Can that be Flaas too? It looks like Flaas got a dose of his own medicine — must have met Big Beth."

It was then that they realized that the horse seemed to be in charge and directing what the Flaas replacement figure was doing. Suddenly the mole vanished and the horse began stomping on the ground like it was trying to step on a very fast spider. The Flaas replacement figure vanished and the blue rabbit hopped toward where the horse was stomping. A large insect suddenly took to wing right from under the horse's hooves. It flew up into the trees and vanished.

The horse began snorting and dancing while the blue rabbit darted around to stay out from under the large mare's feet. The rabbit appeared to glance in their direction, as though he could feel them watching. Aleister had been peaking around the side of the tree. The goose was standing nearly in plain sight, but she was, after all, a goose. The rabbit apparently failed to see Aleister and did not recognize that Crystal was the young woman he had turned into a goose. He turned and began hopping away. The horse snorted again violently and followed.

"I think they're going to have to go back to Flaasland before they can turn back into what they were," said Crystal. "Mrs. Flaas looks pretty good as a Clydesdale. Don't you think?"

Aleister looked around the trees. He could see some white birds perched high up in the trees that seemed to be watching, but that was all they were doing. He turned his attention back to the scene in the park and observed in silence as the rabbit and the Clydesdale disappeared around a corner. "Where is Leonard?" asked Aleister. "He was there and then he was not."

"I think they turned him into some kind of bug," said Crystal sadly. As they talked a large insect descended slowly on the wing and landed on Crystal's back.

"Eeeeooo! What is that," she shrieked, dancing around to try to shake it off. Aleister quickly moved to brush the bug off of her but stopped when he heard the tiny voice calling to him. "Stop! Stop! It's me, Leonard. That low-life son of hundred fathers turned me into a palmetto bug. Then his horse of a wife tried to stomp on me!"

"Great," said Aleister. "Now you're a bug. That's worse than being a mole and now you can't dig burrows for us to sleep in."

"Thanks," said the bug. "All you can think of is yourself. No more burrows to sleep in. What about me? I'm a palmetto bug. I can be eaten by huntsmen spiders and gecko lizards. And not only that, everyone who sees me will try to step on me."

"Look," said Aleister pointing. "There's a green arrow. It's pointing down the road to the east. Let's get out of Print on Demand Land before we're sucked into this madness. You remember what Carleen Alder told us, $50,000 to set up the books for print on demand and then they wouldn't even print any. I have to open a store and sell the book by showing pictures of the cover with a thumbnail synopsis on it. This is crazy. Let's get out of here."

The road east followed the river valley so they didn't have any real hills to climb this time, but the road meandered with the stream so it was not long before the village of Print on Demand was completely out of sight. There was a canopy of shade overhead from the trees and the road had become a dirt track, still heading east. Just after the buildings and factories behind them disappeared, one of the white birds Aleister had seen earlier glided down out of the sky. As he had suspected, it was a chicken. It landed right in front of them, shuffled its feathers, pecked once at an itchy spot on its breast and announced, "You can call me..." the chicken began. But then it noticed the palmetto bug on the goose's back and went for it.

"Stop," cried Aleister, the goose and the bug all at once. "That's Leonard," explained Aleister. "Flaas or his wife or someone turned Leonard into a big palmetto bug."

"Yuck," replied the chicken. "I can't believe I've been reduced to going after bugs. It's sort of a reflex. You know. Chickens love bugs." It preened a feather on one of its wings and continued. "You can call me Bart. My name is Bartemus Tinson but as you can see, Beth Tomawdo turned me into a chicken along with the rest of my fellow poets. I've been elected by the rest of the flock to speak for them."

"Oh my gosh," honked Crystal. "You've formed a Union."

"We formed a Union right after we were changed," replied the chicken. "We call ourselves, the After the Fact Chicken Independence & Liberation Organization."

"Oh no," shrieked Crystal in laughter. "You're the AFCILO, right?" She continued laughing.

"We didn't think it was as funny as that," grumped the chicken. "And you didn't seem to object too much when we saved you from the cannons at Fort Carrion."

"We were very grateful and surprised," said Aleister.

"We stayed with you because you saved us from the butcher shop when you released us from that truck. And we think we have a common purpose. We've overheard you talking and we know you are trying to find a way out of Never Ever Land. We want that too, and we believe that when we leave here we can be changed back into human beings."

"We believe that too," said Aleister. "Do you know anything about a way out of here?"

"No," said the chicken, "but before you arrived, we didn't even have a theory. We thought we'd be stuck here forever, but we know that organization is power. Power is Organization. So, we organized."

"You sound like a radical organizer from Chicago that I used to know. It's true that we have a theory," said Crystal. "We think the evil queen is behind it in some way and we intend to find her and overthrow her. If she's as evil as everyone seems to think, she must have a lot of people in her domain that hate her guts. It should be easy to recruit them into a real army."

"Sedition," said the chicken. "I love it. I think the others will too. We'll try to scout out the area a little bit so we can all know what to expect." The chicken ukbucked once or twice and took to wing.

As it circled once before ascending to join the flock, Crystal commented, "I thought chickens were too heavy to fly. That's why they're always like a ground bird."

The chicken heard what she said. Before beginning its ascent, it squawked once and said, "They starved us on that truck. And besides that, we aren't really chickens. We're poets."

"Ah yes," said Crystal. "I think I once said that."

As they continued along the road, the trees grew thicker and the shadows deepened. Aleister had the distinct feeling that something or someone was watching them from behind. He stopped suddenly several times and looked back but he saw nothing. "Why do you keep doing that?" Crystal asked him.

When he told her, she took to wing, flew back along the road behind them and in less than two minutes she was back. "There's a big lizard back there. It's very long and it's a sort of reddish brown. When I flew over, it kept sticking its tongue out at me and watching me with those beady little eyes, like it wanted to take a bite out of me."

"It was a gecko lizard," said the bug, still riding on Crystal's back. "It was me, he was watching, not her. Gecko lizards eat palmetto bugs. They bite too. I once considered getting one as a pet."

Aleister started looking down the side of the road. Finally, a few feet off the road, he found what he was looking for. It was a heavy stick, about three feet long. It had a ragged broken end and still had most of the bark on it. Armed with this club, he began slowly walking back the way they had come, watching very carefully. The goose followed him on foot at a very respectful distance.

Aleister crept back through the trees, watching each shadow, expecting it to move and jump out at him. Suddenly he heard a scurrying ahead of him and movement in the dry leaves along the side of the road not far off. He froze, turning only his eyes in the direction of the sound. He could see it there, in the shadows of the trees. It was about four feet long, not counting the enormous tail. Its tiny eyes were watching him. He could see the movement on its side, behind its front legs, where its heart was beating. On its left side, behind its heart, there was a green arrow, blinking very faintly. The arrow got his attention. He tried to visualize which direction it was pointing, but as he did, the lizard moved to face in the opposite direction. "Hey," said Aleister. "That won't work. You have an arrow on your side and every time you move it points in a different direction."

"Well what do you expect," said the lizard. "I'm not a tree or a rock. I move around."

"So," said Aleister. "You're another animal that talks. This is a truly a weird place. You're not the first talking lizard I met here, either. I met a talking iguana a while back by the name of Celery."

"I'm not just a lizard," said the lizard. "I'm a published novelist."

"If you're published, what are you doing here in Never Ever Land?"

"My first book was print on demand, but it was back in the days when publishers thought that print on demand would be big because they could sell it easily on the Internet, you know, drop ship and not print the book till it was sold? That was before they started charging like subsidy publishers. They started charging for print set ups because they realized that print on demand books cost more than conventional publishing and no one would buy their books at the higher prices. Subsidies from the authors are the only way they can make any money. No one else would touch my book because they thought I paid to have it printed — it's a print on demand book. Even Amazon called it an 'out of print book.' So, it's Never Ever Land for me. Call me Al, by the way. My name's Allen LeGarto. What's yours?"

By this time, the goose and the bug were closer, but Leonard was whimpering in fear that the gecko would eat him. Aleister recognized the problem and said, "My friend Leonard here has been turned into a bug and he's afraid you'll eat him. Do you eat bugs like other gecko lizards?"

"Good grief no," replied the lizard. "Actually I sort of prefer McDeeps, but I was gaining too much weight, so I had to leave the Valley. I won't be hungry again for weeks. In fact, I was thinking that might make a good new slogan for them. Think if it, 'Eat at McDeeps, no hunger for weeks.' They offer super size coupons for new slogans."

"Bethland is west. We're headed east toward the realms of the evil queen. Maybe you'd be interested in joining us. We plan to find the evil queen and end Never Ever Land."

"I came from the east," answered the lizard. "I came here out of the lands of Mary Death the literary agent. She turned me into a lizard. She thought it was funny because I used to sell insurance."

"If you came from that direction, you might be able to give us some good guidance on the way back. What do you say?"

"As long as I can avoid bumping into Mary death, it sounds great to me. Let's go and put an end for all time to Never Ever Land."

Chapter 10: The Mellow Crick Road

Aleister and his friends continued the trek through the forest, now with the lizard as part of their crew. They had to be careful about not getting too close behind the lizard because, as he walked, his tail swished back and forth. If they got too close, the lizard's tail would sweep their feet right out from under them. They had slept under some bushes along side the path. The dirt clinging to his clothing and skin made Aleister feel very uncomfortable. As he walked, he continually brushed at his clothing, trying to get rid of the dead leaf pieces that were sticking all over him.

"What are you doing?" asked the goose in frustration. "You keep beating at yourself."

"I'm trying to brush off the dirt," snapped Aleister.

"Try just imagining that none of it is there. Forget about it. You can get clean again when you have the chance, but beating at yourself like that isn't going to accomplish anything."

Aleister stopped walking. "Okay." He knew he was annoying everyone and wanted to be appeasing. "I'll try that." He closed his eyes, held his head high and after a minute passed, he opened his eyes and continued walking. He carefully kept his eyes straight ahead, not daring to look at his soiled clothing.

"Wow," said the lizard. "Look at him now."

"No dirt," piped the bug.

"Where did the dirt all go?" Crystal asked with obvious surprise.

"What do you mean — where did the dirt go?" snapped Aleister. "I imagined it away."

"But Aleister," the goose whispered. "The dirt is really all gone."

Aleister couldn't resist the temptation. "I don't believe it," he snapped. He quickly looked down at his shirt and pants. Instantly, they were covered again with dead leaf pieces and spots of dirt, worse than before. "I see nothing different." His sullen tones matched the dirt in his cloths.

"But it was all gone after you closed your eyes and imagined it away, as you put it," insisted the lizard.

"Try it again," Crystal coached, "but this time, don't look down again."

"This is pointless," Aleister complained but he resigned himself to the experiment. Once more, the leaves and dirt vanished and his shirt looked as though it had just come from the laundry.

"See? See? It works," cried the goose with glee. "Don't look at it this time," she added.

"This is too weird," the bug called out to them. "He can't make it just disappear than reappear like that. It's either there or it's not."

"Yeah, right," Crystal laughed. "And you're either a cockroach or a writer named Leonard DeMolier. Which is it?"

"I'm not a cockroach," exclaimed the bug. "I'm a palmetto bug."

"A palmetto bug's just a Florida cockroach," grinned Crystal. "And it answers my question. I'm not a goose. I'm a girl named Crystal Goose-worthy." With that Crystal closed her eyes and while the others watched in amazement, she became herself once again, if only for a few seconds. As soon as she opened her eyes, she was a goose again.

"Maybe we better put these discoveries on hold for a few minutes," suggested Aleister. "Look up ahead."

They had arrived at the end of the forest. The land ahead of them stretched arid and flat into the distance. Only scrubby little bushes and sparse grass covered the ground. The plain had as its introduction, another intersection. The road split into five directions with one big sign sprouting arrows all over it. The labels on the arrows indicated the paths to Bethland, Flaassland, Print on Demand Land and others. The main thoroughfare had mud brick pavement, reinforced with bits of straw sticking out of every brick. This road bore its own sign saying, "The Mellow Crick Road, to the land of the Evil Queen and the dread domains beyond." Underneath it said, "Abandon all Hope, Ye Who Enter Here."

"Now what?" All of them shared Aleister's frustration and confusion.

"I think that's already been decided," the goose muttered in grim determination. "We're going to the lands of the Evil Queen."

"What about the warning?" Aleister objected, pointing a the sign.

"That's just literary gobbledygook," the lizard answered in disgust. "It's a quote from Dante's *Inferno* and I think we should ignore it. I came from these lands. Ahead of us, long before we get to the lands of the Evil Queen lies the domains of Merry Death. She's the one who turned me into a lizard."

As they followed the Mellow Crick Road, the goose and the lizard kept glancing at Aleister's clothing to see if there was still any dirt on it. Aleister himself refused to look at it again. Sometimes when the others looked, the clothing was clean. Other times, it still had the dirt and leaves on it. Finally, Crystal stopped looking. Aleister forgot about it, and the clothing remained clean.

Their sheer determination won out over unbending tediousness of The Mellow Crick Road. They kept going. In time, Aleister stopped. "What's that up ahead?"

They all strained their eyes trying to see what he squinted at. About half a mile ahead, something stood over the road, like a small bridge. "I think it looks more like some sort of small deck over the road," suggested the goose. "What do you guys think?"

"I think it looks like a giant huntsman spider," the bug shuddered. "It's there hunting and it wants to eat me."

"It looks big enough that it could eat me, even," remarked the goose.

"I've seen pictures of big spiders fighting with lizards." The lizard began backing away.

"I don't like spiders much more than I like roaches," announced Aleister. "Let's get a little closer and see if it talks like most of the other creatures we've met in this place."

The party continued toward the east along the Mellow Crick Road, but they slowed their pace considerably. As they grew closer, they could see the spider's antennae waving above its head. Its mandibles were moving back and forth as though it were chewing something, or worse yet, wishing it had something to chew. It was a hairy spider, except for its legs. They were long and rubbery looking, as though the spider could move at lightning speed, if it wanted to do that. All eight of its eyes were obviously following them as they approached.

It was only after they had drawn much closer that Aleister could see a large case beside the spider on the ground. On the side of the case it said, "Advanced release, Merry Death, Literary Agent."

"It looks like you're selling books," Aleister greeted the spider when he was close enough for it to hear but not close enough, in Aleister's judgement, to jump on him.

"And the tourists that don't buy 'em," the spider replied, "I eat. It looks to me like I have four sales coming up, or a nice dinner. Which is it?"

"We have a long way to go," Aleister remonstrated. "We can't carry a lot of books with us. Please let us pass."

"If you show up in the lands of Merry Death without any of her books, she just might turn you into a spider and make you sell books for her. Can't you just buy one of them?"

The spider's pleading tones gave Aleister some confidence that he hadn't been feeling. "None of us has any money," Aleister answered. "We spent it all on reading fees with Ronald Flaass over in Flaassland. What are your books about anyway?"

"They're something you're going to need if you intend to travel very far on this road. It's called *A Detailed tour of the Mellow Crick Road*. It was written by Rodman Stinton's computer. He's a literary agent from Boston and Mary is trying to help him get started here in Never Ever Land."

Aleister looked at the case full of books. Then he looked back at the spider and understood that this was another writer, who had been turned into some awful creature by yet another unscrupulous, perceived authority on literary prowess. "I've noticed," began Aleister, "that when someone we look up to, believe in and trust tells we are good at something or bad at something, we believe them. If they tell us we're a palmetto bug or a spider, we believe them and actually become what they told us we are. It seems that we become what we believe we are. To become something else, all we seem to have to do is change our minds. I bet you weren't always a spider. What are you?"

"Well, now that you mention it," began the spider. "I used to sell Bibles and dictionaries to schools. Then I wrote a book on selling techniques. I went to Merry Death to try to get her to be my literary agent. She led me through her mirror into this place and told me I was as pitiful as a bug eating spider, and wa la... I was suddenly what I am now. You're right, I guess. My name is Angelica Jager. Jager means hunter. Maybe that's why she made me a huntsman spider. What do you think?"

By this time, Crystal and the other two had come close enough to hear what was going on. "This is really strange," she ventured. "This is a little like what we were talking about just a few minutes ago. When Aleister imagined that his clothes were clean, they were. When he forgot and quit imagining, his clothes were dirty again."

"That's nonsense." Aleister refused to consider the idea, although he had just explained the same thought to the spider. "My clothes are still dirty. Just look at them."

They all did, and just as Aleister had said, his shirt and pants were covered with flecks of dead leaves and dirt from the ground where he had slept last night. "And Angelica here not only just looks like a spider, she is a spider. Merry Death must be as bad as Flaass."

"I don't care what you say," Crystal honked rebelliously. "I'm not really a goose and Leonard isn't really a roach."

"Palmetto bug!" corrected Leonard.

"And I'm not a gecko," the lizard denounced his chosen reality. "I'm a published novelist. My name is Allen LeGarto. All this is nonsense. Flaass, Tomawda and Death have to be some kind of wizards. If they weren't, we'd still all be people."

"Merry Death sure turned me into a spider," the spider announced. "Just look at me."

"Why don't you leave your case of books here," suggested Aleister. "Forget about Merry Death and selling her books. We're on a quest to find the evil queen whose name no one knows because everyone's afraid to mention it. We believe she's the one behind this Never Ever Land foolishness and we intend to put a stop to it. Why don't you join us?"

"The evil queen?" parroted the spider. Her tone took on a reverent quality as she added, "She's the one they call 'you know who,' over in Deathland. Everyone's afraid of her. Her lands lie way beyond the domains of Merry Death. Going there to find her sounds pretty crazy to me."

"If she's the one behind this," answered the goose, "then we have to go there to end Never Ever Land."

"What else do you have to do?" demanded the lizard. "Are you going to spend the rest of your life selling tour books on the Mellow Crick Road? Let's go."

Aleister could hear distant clucking. He looked up into the sky. Following his gaze, they all looked up. High in the sky they could see a large flock of white birds headed east above the road. "What're you all looking at up there?" asked the spider.

"We're not alone," smiled Aleister. "They're with us."

Now they were five and a motley crew they were, no two of them alike. The road went straight east. There were wild fields on both sides of the road. No farmer had cultivated this section and it seemed to go on for miles. In the distance, Aleister could see a line of trees, as though a stream meandered through the area. "Angelica," Aleister addressed the spider. "You've been through here before. What's in the line of trees?"

The spider didn't answer at first, as though it was considering what it wanted to say. Then it answered. "That is the land of J. Anastasia Punch, an interesting and engaging woman. She was once a literary

agent herself, but she subcontracted to Merry Death for a joint enter-
prise and she's been lost here ever since. If we find her, I think you may
like her."

Chapter 11: The Domain of Merry Death

The land the Mellow Creek Road stretched through grew more hilly. The denseness of the forest increased as they continued the trek toward the home of the Evil Queen. As the hills grew steeper, the road became more winding and Aleister feared what might lie beyond the next turn, turn after turn. The entourage now consisted of five on the ground and many chickens occasionally seen on the wing. The palmetto bug, Leonard DeMolier, took to wing from the back of the goose and landed on Aleister's shoulder. Aleister resisted the instinct to swat it. Instead he simply asked, "What's up, Leonard?"

"I don't mean to stir up anything," he spoke softly. "But huntsman spiders don't have antennas. That's not a real huntsman. In fact, spiders don't have antennas. She's some kind of eight legged bug."

Before Aleister could answer, they heard a loud whirring in the air, punctuated with high-pitched shouts. The group halted its progress, suddenly tense and ready to run or fight. The whirring grew closer and they could now make out words.

"No! No! Leave me alone! Go away!"

From around the bend, ahead of them appeared a large dragonfly with a mockingbird in hot pursuit. The voice was from the dragonfly. When it saw Aleister and his friends it darted toward them and ducked behind Aleister. The mockingbird pulled up suddenly, coming to what would have been a screeching halt if it had not taken place in the air. It then flitted to a tree limb just over Aleister's head.

"Oh. I remember you," grimaced the mockingbird. "You've come a long way for traveling on the ground. Are you still planning on killing the Evil Queen?" it asked with a chuckling snort.

Aleister glanced back at his friends, then returning his gaze up to the mockingbird he replied, "If that's what it takes to end Never Ever Land, yes."

"She'll change you," chirped the mockingbird. "If you make it past all those who defend the border, you will never ever return to Never Ever land."

"Why would we want to come back here?" Aleister demanded.

"Some spend their whole lives here." The bird lifted off, landing on a twig slightly lower and closer to Aleister. "It's not such a bad place, unless you want to get published. Why not get a job and stay?"

"Because I don't want to be a goose anymore," honked Crystal. "Leonard doesn't want to be a bug and Angelica doesn't want to be a spider."

"Don't forget about me," interjected the lizard. "I'd rather still be selling insurance than stuck here. What has any of us got to lose?"

"Don't forget about me," shouted the dragonfly. "I don't want to be a bug either."

"Who are you?" Crystal asked the dragonfly sympathetically.

"My name is Lee Ann. I wrote the book on the history of old jails and got trapped in Print on Demand Land. Big Beth turned me into a dragonfly because my email address has 'dragonfly' in it. She was mad because I wasn't huge and I refused to eat at McDeeps. Now I perch on the ends of fishing poles and look beautiful — except when I'm trying to avoid being lunch for a mockingbird!"

"Yeah. What's the idea, mockingbird?" demanded Crystal.

"Give me a break," the mockingbird complained. "Mockingbirds eat bugs. She's a bug. Let me at her!"

"Just hold on, here," asserted Aleister. "None of us are going to eat any of us. You must be the same mockingbird I met before because you knew we were looking for the Evil Queen."

"Don't change the subject," the mockingbird chirped angrily. "Just get out of my way."

"No so fast," the lizard chimed in.

"You'll have to get through all of us," added the spider. "You might notice that between the lizard here and myself, we might just eat you!"

"Enough!" Aleister cut in loudly. "Who are you, mockingbird?"

"I'm a real mockingbird. I was hatched just west of here in Flaassland. My parents were writers. Flaass accused them of plagiarizing one of his books. That's why he made them mockingbirds, for mocking his computer's work. What's wrong with imitating a successful formula? Everybody does it and for the most part, if they don't do it, they get nowhere. Agents and publishers all insist that writers follow formulas. Look at Flaass! Look at Beth! Look at Merry Death!"

"So, you're telling us that you have always been a mockingbird?"

"Yes," the mockingbird chirped proudly. "And I like being a mockingbird. I like Never Ever Land. I think you're crazy for wanting to leave but I'm glad I told you how to find the Evil Queen. She'll have you for breakfast."

"Come here," Crystal whispered to the dragonfly. "Duck under my wing and you'll be safe till that awful bird goes away."

"Do you think he sees me?" Leonard the palmetto bug whispered to Aleister from his shoulder.

Having overheard, the mockingbird stated coldly, "I don't eat palmetto bugs." It then took to flight and disappeared around the bend in the road from where he had come.

"That was close," moaned the dragonfly as it crept out from under the goose's wing. "I thought I was a goner for sure."

"I can't imagine not wanting to get out of here," volunteered Leonard the palmetto bug. "Can you believe it? That bird said he was born and raised as a mockingbird in Never Ever Land."

"Let's move on," Aleister suggested. "Lee Ann, can you tell us what to expect ahead of us?"

The dragonfly took to flight and landed on Aleister's shoulder. "Not far ahead is the Village of La-La-Land. The mayor is known as Doctor Pangloss. He's a retired philosophy professor who wrote a book called *All is for the Best in This Best of All Possible Worlds*. Now he edits two magazines called *News Speak* and *Rhyme Magazine*. They specialize in telling people what Pangloss thinks they want to hear and nothing that he thinks they don't want to hear. Beyond La-La-Land is Death Valley Proper, the home of Merry Death. Beyond that are the Borderlands lying between Never Ever Land and the Realms of the Evil Queen."

"Have you seen all these places?" asked Aleister.

"I've been everywhere except the Borderlands."

"La-La-Land sounds bizarre."

"It is," replied the dragonfly. "Quite bizarre, but you'll see. The people there actually go for all that. *Rhyme Magazine* named Ronald Flaass 'Man of the Year,' last year. He even took off his rabbit suit for the photograph," she laughed.

The six rounded the last bend and started down the last hill, entering La-La-Land. Ahead, on the edge of the village, they saw a café with outside tables and a canopy overhead. People sat around sipping iced tea. Some chatted happily while others read magazines. As the unusual party walked past, no one even looked up, as though seeing a giant spider with antennas, a four-foot long gecko lizard (not counting the tail), accompanied by a goose and a young man with a bug on each shoulder was the most common sight one could see. As they passed, one of the people at a table stated loudly, "It is certainly a beautiful day."

Aleister looked up at the sky noticing gathering clouds. "Looks to me like it's going to rain," he casually commented.

The person at the table asserted, "It's not going to rain. It's a beautiful day."

"But look at the clouds." Aleister pointed.

"The man frowned, looked around at his companions who were also frowning. As drops of rain began falling on them and making a rat-a-tat sound on the canopy, he insisted, "It's not going to rain. It's a beautiful day."

"Excuse me," Aleister interjected, stepping under the canopy. "I think I'll just step in here for a moment until it stops raining."

Before he could finish what he was saying, all the people at the café who heard this exchange, put their fingers in their ears and shouted at the top of their voices, "La-la-la-la-la-la-la-la-la-la."

The dragonfly started laughing. Crystal the goose looked from one to another, then at Aleister and then at the laughing dragonfly and she started laughing too. Aleister was a bit nonplussed. The blank look on his face spurred on their laughter. All the while, the people in the café continued with their La-la-la-la-la-la-la-la-la-la-ing. Finally Aleister began smiling and then laughing. He threw his hands up in the air and shouted loudly over the breaking thunder from above, "It sure is a beautiful day!"

It was then that Aleister noticed the open magazine lying on a table in front of him. At the top, on the right side of the page was the title, "*News Speak*'s Weather Page." Down below the headline predicted "Beautiful Weather Today." Beneath that, a picture depicted a man standing in a bucket and trying to lift himself by the handle. The lead for the article was "Churchill was Wrong."

The La-la-la-ing stopped. The people in the café removed their fingers from their ears and they resumed their happy conversations and their reading. The rain stopped and Aleister's party moved on. As they left, Aleister heard one man saying loudly, "*News Speak* says it. I believe it and that settles it." Aleister and the goose started laughing again.

As they passed through the community, Aleister noticed shops of all sorts with happy smiling, wet people everywhere. As they approached a clothing shop, a lady emerged just as a medium sized dog came by. The dripping wet dog stopped in front of the lady and shook itself. Water flew, spraying off of the dog, soaking the woman. She leaped back in horror as the muddy drops stained her dress. Aleister couldn't resist saying in passing, "I'm certainly glad there won't be any rain today."

Crystal starting laughing again as the lady smiled and recited, "It certainly is a beautiful day. Isn't it?"

The next shop was a bookstore. Aleister was eager to see what they had for sale there, but as he approached, he noticed several large racks of books under their awning, just outside the door, under a sign that said, "Remainders." The sign above the door said, "All our books sell like hot cakes." Aleister looked into the shop through the open door and saw only empty shelves.

He walked in and was greeted by the shopkeeper whom he liked immediately because the man was shorter than 5'7". The shopkeeper wore thick glasses, had thin hair combed straight back and a number 2 pencil stuck behind one ear. "Any new releases?" Aleister asked him.

"All sold out," the man smiled, looking up at Aleister. "Check out our remainders, right outside the door. We got some of them only yesterday. Everything sells so fast here, ya know."

As this exchange took place, the dragonfly took to flight off of Aleister's shoulder after whispering, "Watch this." She flew over the counter, and six feet to the right where she landed on a large piece of paper lying next to an open envelope. At the top of the paper were the words, "Eviction Notice," followed in smaller print beneath it, "Rent payment default."

Aleister wondered idly if the man would seek a job with Literary Agent Flaass. "It sure is a beautiful day. Isn't it?"

"Oh yes," the man replied. "And business is booming."

On the way out of town, they passed a school. Since it was such a beautiful day, outside classes were in order. A middle aged *haus frau* with a baggy print dress led the class. She was soaked to the skin. The children seated on the muddy ground dripped from the recent downpour. As they sat there, the teacher could be heard as far as the street saying, "Put your index finger in your right cheek like so," and she demonstrated. "Now say, 'it's such a beautiful day. La-la-la-la-la-la-la...'"

"Lee Ann," Aleister spoke confidentially. "You are right. This is a bizarre place. I wonder what we'll find in the land of Merry Death.

"This IS the land of Merry Death. It's just the first township." The Mellow Creek Road stretched out before them. "This isn't the end of La-La Land," the dragonfly continued. That was just the beginning."

Before she finished speaking, they spotted a cottage ahead on the right. It was a small, simple affair with a low, hip roof and a walkway from the front door to the road. A man stood in front of the house in a large bucket. Half bent over, he tugged at the handle of the bucket. He was sweating. His shirt was moist from it, his hat stained and his face flushed. The group paused to watch him. He stood straight up for a moment, wiped his brow on his sleeve and returned to his labor, tugging at the handle of the bucket. He was a short man, taller than Aleister of course, but short. A woman came out of the cottage, with a copy of the latest issue of *News Speak* in one hand, folded open to the weather page. She was wearing a plain dress with a full skirt and a white apron, stained with whatever she had cooking inside. "You don't have to prove *everything*, George," she told the man. "If it says it here," she lifted the magazine toward him on the word , 'here.' "Then it's true," she continued.

"I know. I know," George answered her. "I just want to see for myself."

"May I ask what you are doing?" Crystal muttered loudly enough to be heard.

"I am proving that what the article in *News Speak* says is true, that a man can stand in a bucket and lift himself by the handle."

"He's been working at it all morning," the woman's voice expressed exasperation.

"Well I know it can be done," insisted George. "I just haven't pulled hard enough yet, or I haven't tried often enough yet. If *News Speak* says it, I believe, and that settles it."

"If it's all settled, then why try to prove it?" asked Crystal innocently.

"I am an economist," the man snapped. "I am proving that Winston Churchill's statement was wrong. This is the illustration he used. I am certain that a bankrupt economy can lift itself out of bankruptcy by tripling its debt load. It only makes sense. Even *Rhyme Magazine* supports the theory."

"Let's go," urged Aleister. "We've spent enough time in La-La-Land." As they resumed their journey, Aleister called out to the man, "Certainly is a beautiful day. Isn't it? A bit wet, perhaps, but beautiful."

The man stood straight up in his bucket. He took off his hat and wiped his brow again with a big smile. "It certainly is a beautiful day, and it's not supposed to rain, so it won't."

Chapter 12: La-La-Land

By mid-afternoon Aleister's legs felt weary. He liked the company just fine but for a while they were annoying him by constantly singing "Follow the Mellow Crick Road." The surface mud brick surface still had bits of straw sticking out. The bricks remained a bit slippery from the rain earlier, but by noon they had pretty much dried out. The terrain had remained heavily wooded until only an hour ago when they emerged into what seemed an endless, rolling meadow. Ahead in the distance, Aleister could see a large clump of trees that stretched out of sight beyond the hills of the meadow.

Lee Ann the dragonfly flitted about among the Queen's Ann Lace and the other wild flowers in the vast meadow. Crystal the goose waddled along behind Aleister who still carried Leonard the palmetto bug on his shoulder. Allen the lizard came along slowly, in the distance behind them, swishing his tail as he moved. Angelica the spider sped ahead of the group from time to time and then waited while they approached. Aleister anticipated the refreshment of the shade trees ahead, but as they neared the trees, he began to feel apprehensive.

When they entered the large grove, they slowed their pace. The spider waited just under the trees. "I haven't found anything remarkable in here," Angelica told them. "It's a bit gloomy and there's Spanish moss everywhere. Ahead, the road splits again. You'll see."

"Look there! Look there," Leonard began ecstatically. "Look at the sign." He indicated a small sign, almost out of sight beside a large clump of dog fennel.

The sign read, "Pitt Falls and Coulter's Lounge."

"Maybe they have Coulter's Candy," the palmetto bug offered happily. "Have you ever tasted that stuff? Let's go in there. I want some."

"It sounds like a little resort of some kind," suggested Crystal. "And maybe there is a river with a falls. That would be nice to see."

"We have been walking all day," groaned Aleister. "Maybe this would be a good place to spend the night, then get an early start in the morning. Whadya think?"

The path narrowed, descending through a deepening ravine. A thin creek appeared at the bottom, fed by a small spring near the top of the path. The earth still felt soft under their feet, from the rain earlier, but pine needle layering protected them from the mud underneath. They covered several hundred yards before the path broadened again and leveled into a large, partly open area, shaded under huge oaks. Two buildings stood at the far end of the shaded meadow, along the edge of a stream flowing behind them. Both were clapboard cottages with open porches and a single door in the center, framed by windows on either side. Paint peeled from the walls of both buildings, exposing faded gray wood. Their rusted, tin roofs overhung the outside walls by a foot. The two cottages stood about thirty yards apart. Above the door on the cottage to their right, a sign announced "Coulter's Lounge." The other one had a sign, "Rest for the Weary."

At the palmetto bug's urging, they went first to Coulter's Lounge. There, a lovely, tall young woman with long blonde hair and a husky voice greeted them warmly. The large retail area included a small café at one end, a gift shop displaying mostly books at the other and an entrance, half way between, sporting a sign above the door saying, "Museum."

"Let's look at the books," suggested Aleister.

"I'd rather go through the museum," Crystal answered. "Let's do that first."

"You know me," the palmetto bug chuckled. "I want some Coulter's Candy. Let's get some of that then eat it while we go through the museum."

Aleister and the bug took a seat at the café counter. Leonard still rode on his shoulder. Aleister asked the young woman, now behind the counter, "My friend Leonard, here on my shoulder would like some Coulter's Candy and I'd like a BLT on whole wheat if you have it. Do you mind if Leonard rests on the counter while he eats his candy. He's not really a palmetto bug. He's a writer who..."

"I know," cut in the young lady. "It looks like the work of Flaasss or Tomawdo. Of course he can rest on the counter, but I hope he doesn't eat my book." As she said this she placed a book in front of him titled,

How to talk to a Literary Agent (If You Must), and subtitled *Coulter's Candy.*

It was only then Aleister noticed the name tag she was wearing on her blouse. It said, "Culture Warrior."

"Call me CW for short," she told him with a smile. "I'm, uh, sort of a missionary. I try to bring Political Fundamentalists into the light but in Never Ever Land it's a hopeless chore, especially so near La-La-Land. We have to be careful what we talk about inside here, by the way. The place is *bugged.*"

Aleister looked around and could see insects crawling around the corners and walls. "Why don't you get rid of them? This is disgusting."

"They aren't alive," chortled CW. "They're mechanical listening devices." With a toss of her head, she shook a strand of hair out of her face. "They follow me all over the place. It's the only way Merry Death will let me *have* this small business. Let's go outside to the deck. We can have better privacy from the bugs there."

A large deck in the rear of the building provided a beautiful view of the stream with marsh and meadow beyond. The spider and lizard waited in front of the cottage, dozing. Lee Ann the dragonfly stayed with Crystal. Aleister and CW took seats on the deck where picnic tables and benches made this a nicer place to sit and eat than the counter inside. CW sipped a cup of tea with obvious pleasure. Leonard sat on the table munching a tiny piece of pecan pie. As Aleister took his second bite, he looked up in surprise.

"Look at that, will you," he muttered in amazement.

A man was floating by, three feet above the creek, wearing coveralls, thick glasses and a golf cap that said "Merry Death for President." He was standing in a bucket that he held suspended, by its handle.

"That's impossible," Aleister whispered in amazement.

CW started chuckling as she tossed her hair out of her face again. "He's been floating up and down the stream all morning."

"But... how can he do that?"

"He can't, except in Never Ever Land. He lives about a mile downstream. Watch this."

She stood and walked to the rail overlooking the creek. As the man came closer, she called out to him, "Hi there, Arlan. Sure is a beautiful day. Isn't it?"

The man looked up with a wide smile on his face. Letting go of the handle of the bucket, he tried to stand up to answer, when to his surprise he fell into the creek with a great splash. He found himself neck deep in the stream with the bucket floating beside him. Aleister's laughter almost made him choke on his bite of sandwich. The palmetto bug had rolled over on his back, holding his stomach. CW called out to the man, "You okay Arlan? Need some help?"

The man was sputtering with rage. He reached out beside him and grabbed his golf cap that was beginning to sink and slapped it back on his head. It was full of water that doused him thoroughly when he turned it to put it on. His glasses were splattered with drops of water and it's doubtful that he could see much at all. He was swearing viciously and to report what he said, it has to be cleaned up. He said something like, "You horrible person! You never speak to me, ever. But now that you could see I needed my concentration..."

Aleister was laughing again, so hard that he missed the rest of what the man was saying. CW left the deck's rail and returned to her seat next to Aleister. The grin on her face said it all. "People around here don't much like me," she said through her chortling. "I guess I'm not that good a missionary. Sometimes I have to let them learn the hard way."

"You called them Political Fundamentalists. What do you mean by that?" Aleister took another bite of his sandwich and wiped a couple of tears from his eyes, that had formed from his laughter.

"Well, think of it like this. Have you ever tried to make a fundamentalist actually *THINK*? It's impossible. They are totally buried within the framework of what ever dogma they have chosen, be it Islam, Christianity, Ba'Hai — whatever. Thinking *about it* is not an option. Their only option is thinking about *how to defend it.*" She took a sip of her tea, swept a strand of hair out of her face and continued. "That's why I call some of these folks Political Fundamentalists. How long have you been in the realm of Merry Death?"

"Just a day or so. Why?"

"How many times have you heard someone say, '*News Speak* said it. I believe it and that settles it'?"

"At least three times, I guess."

"Point made," affirmed CW.

෬   ෮

With the shadows growing longer and the sun sinking into the sky, the friends re-assembled in front of the building. CW assured Aleister that bunks were available in the cottage labeled "Rest for The Weary," so, together, they headed in that direction.

"The museum is wonderful," Crystal reported as she pecked at an itch under her left wing.

"They had Indian stuff," the dragonfly chimed in. "There were arrow heads, pottery. They even had an exhibit showing an archeological dig, near here."

"What did they find?" asked the lizard.

"All kinds of stuff," answered the goose. "Bones, pottery, arrowheads and..."

"There were clay tablets," interjected the dragonfly. "They were in cuneiform. How was the food?"

"It was fine, but when Leonard asked for some Coulter's Candy, CW gave him a book called *How to Talk to A Literary Agent (If You Must)*. He didn't eat it, so she gave him a piece of pie."

Suddenly the ground gave way beneath them and the party of six all found themselves in a pit at least ten feet deep with straight up and down sides. After the shrieking subsided, Crystal looked around and announced, "This is no problem for me." She opened her wings and flew out of the hole.

"Looks good to me," echoed Leonard. He spread his bug wings and lifted off, followed closely by Lee Ann the dragonfly.

"That leaves the three of us," observed Aleister, looking around.

"Speak for yourself," muttered the spider as she walked up the side of the hole.

Just then, Aleister heard a tiny voice somewhere beneath him calling out frantically, "Help! Help!"

Above, Aleister could hear a flurry of wings. He looked up to discover a huge flock of chickens descending on the yard. Looking around at his feet, Aleister continued trying to discover the source of the voice. Nothing could be seen but loose dirt with a few rocks and roots. The latex gloves were gone and his reluctance to go fishing around in the dirt with his bare hands was very intense, but at the continued pleading of the voice, he did so. Shortly, he came up with a very muddy, large seed. The voice stopped but only for a moment.

"Thank you for rescuing me," the seed cried out. "I was buried alive."

"What did you find?" asked Allen the lizard.

"Looks like a seed of some kind."

"A peach pit, to be precise," retorted the seed.

"Don't tell me you're another writer," Aleister muttered.

"A poet, actually," the seed informed him. "My name is Jonathon Peach. Flaass turned me into a real peach and sold me Beth Tomawda. She ate my flesh and me gave me to Merry Death who planted me in this place. 'Good place for a peach tree,' she told me."

"How did the hole get here?" asked Aleister. "Did someone try to trap us?"

"Oh that..." muttered the peach pit. "There were some Preditors here from Flaassland. They dug the pit to trap some escapees, they said.

They forgot I was planted here. Would those escapees be you?"

"Probably," Aleister answered. "That explains why the sign on the road said, 'Pitt Falls.' How soon do you think they'll be back to check their trap?"

"They've been coming around just about every day. In fact you just missed them. They stopped just a few hours ago."

"Do you think they may have planted more of these for us on our path east?"

"They probably did. If you continue east, you should have a care about where you step."

Crystal called out from above, "I'm glad we found Jonathon Peach. Why aren't you a chicken like the rest of the poets?"

"They landed in the Valley of the Shadow of Beth. I landed in Flaassland, I guess. Who is that above who recognized my name?"

"I'm Crystal Gooseworthy," she answered glancing over her right wing. "Here comes CW with some rope. We'll get you three out of there directly.

Chapter 13: Money in, Garbage out

First light enabled them to see well enough to find their way back to the Mellow Crick Road. "Jonathon," Crystal began, a bit breathless from the climb. "What time of day do the Preditors usually come to check their trap?"

"I can't really say," the peach pit answered from Aleister's pocket. "I was always underground when they showed up and I couldn't tell if it was night or day. As you know, a peach pit doesn't have a lot of locomotion so I couldn't exactly, ya know, stick my nose out and take a look."

"So, they could show up at any time, right?" from Leonard the palmetto bug.

"And you don't know if they had winged monkeys with them or not either, do you?" inquired Crystal.

"Or the Color Cop or the Boxhead Cop. There isn't much you can tell us, is there?" Aleister continued the questioning.

"Nope. Sorry," came the muffled reply from Aleister's pocket.

At the East edge of the small forest, they found another crossroads. This time they had only two choices. The sign pointing to the right said, "To the Borderlands and The Domain of the Evil Queen." The other pointed to the left indicating "Death Valley and the home of Merry Death."

"I don't think we want to meet Merry Death. Do any of you?" Aleister ventured.

"No, no," came replies from all.

As they continued their trek toward the Borderlands and the Evil Queen, their tones grew more somber. They knew they were beginning to get close. "It looks like we only have to make it across the rest of Merry Death's Domain and we'll be at the Borderlands," the palmetto bug observed. "It's been a long journey, just as the turtle said. Remember the turtle?" he asked Aleister.

"A chapter a day, that's the way. No more. No less. No more. No less," Aleister mimicked the turtle's drawn out tones and words.

"We should be okay as long as we say it correctly, aye?" Leonard snickered.

"Only if you're in France," smirked Aleister. "They say it doesn't matter how you say a thing in France, as long as you pronounce it correctly. In England, it's grammar grammar grammar, but the pronunciation doesn't seem to matter. I read they have over eighty major dialects in the United Kingdom and in that, they include American."

"Be nice," objected the bug. "Remember my name is DeMolier and that's definitely from France."

"Yeah, cool it on your ethnic slurs," demanded Crystal. "My name is Gooseworthy and that is definitely from the U.K. Enough already."

"Sorry," Aleister promised. "So what are we going to do once we actually get to the Borderlands? We don't know what we're going to find there, or if we're going to be attacked again."

"I think if we can avoid the Preditors and the winged monkeys we should be okay," Crystal brought the subject back to center. "But the only thing we have going for us in that department is they don't know where to look for us."

"We do know they're still trying to find us," Aleister offered.

"True," agreed the palmetto bug. "But we haven't seen any of them in several days and when we last saw Flaass, he had been turned into a real, blue rabbit."

"My guess," began Aleister, "is that he had to go back to Flaassland to get himself straightened out, if he can even do that himself. And Gertrude is probably still a big horse in a sleeveless tee-shirt."

"That was funny to see." If Crystal had had lips instead of a goose's beak, she would have smiled. "I guess I have to admit that Big Beth has a sense of humor."

"I don't think so," the dragonfly objected. "I bet the chicken/poets don't think so either and neither does Jonathon who is now just a peach pit because Beth ate him."

Angelica the spider had run far ahead again as she had been doing the last day or so. This time she wasn't waiting for them to catch up. She was coming back on the run. When she arrived within earshot, she breathlessly told them, "There are a lot of people ahead and there's trouble."

Continuing east, the road leveled off and became almost perfectly straight. The terrain, just a step above arid desert provided life for only succulents like cactus and thin grasses. In the distance, Aleister saw a large tower but much closer than that he saw people on both sides of the road with no one actually on the road. As the group drew closer, Aleister could hear shouting and he could see that people on either side of the road were throwing things at each other as they shouted.

Aleister suddenly heard a flutter of wings. He looked up apprehensively, expecting to see winged monkeys. Instead, he saw a large white chicken descending. "Hello Bartemus," he recognized the appointed spokes-chicken for the chicken union. "What's going on up ahead? Do you know?"

Bartemus landed on the ground in front of Aleister, shuffled his feathers, clucked once and answered. "It's some kind of big argument," reported the chicken. "They're all so angry they won't even talk to each other. All they do is throw mud and rotten vegetables back and forth."

The chicken scratched at the ground, cocked its head to one side to inspect its scratchings and pecked at something two or three times. Aleister didn't see what the chicken/poet was pecking at.

"How long does this go on?" asked Aleister.

The chicken stopped pecking and glanced up at Aleister as though it had lost its train of thought for a moment. Then it said, "Oh yes. It stretches on like this for a couple of miles, then you come to the tower. After the tower, it stretches on a few more miles. Then you come to the desert."

The chicken resumed scratching and pecking at the ground. "What are you eating?" asked Aleister.

The chicken looked up again with the demeanor that he was about to answer a stupid question. "Ants, of course. They are very high protein and quite good for the constitution. I used to like them coated in chocolate, but they're just as good fresh."

"Oh gawd," muttered Crystal. "Eeoo."

"Ants indeed," the lizard answered thoughtfully. "I'll have to give it a try."

Leonard the palmetto bug, slipped quietly underneath Aleister's collar, out of sight. The dragonfly took to wing, staying carefully out of the chicken's reach.

Aleister rolled his eyes, swept his hand across his forehead, took a deep breath and asked, "What is the tower used for?"

The chicken stopped scratching again, looked back up at Aleister and said, "Oh," as though Aleister's question was yet another unwelcome distraction. "It's some kind of government building. It's silly, really. It has only one door and it's marked, 'Entrance.' Once a person goes in, they never ever come out again. I heard, some have been there more than forty years and the building has no windows, no television, no phones. They have no contact with the outside world. All they do is raise taxes and pass laws that meddle with the affairs of others. Haven't you ever wondered why there is no industry in Never Ever Land and people like us are trying to get out?"

Aleister took another deep breath and said, "This is no time to talk about politics. How do we get past that obstruction? Is that going to be a problem?"

"We chickens are going to fly over it and wait for you on the other side. We wanted to recommend that you try to circle this mess but if you do that you might get lost in the extremes of this wasteland. The safest way is probably straight down the middle of the road. If you stray to either the right or the left you might get sucked into the conflicts. Either way, you're probably going to get mud all over you because that's what they're throwing at each other, for the most part."

"And if we're in the middle, we're going to get hit with it. I understand," Aleister thoughtfully answered trying to think of a solution. Then he added as the chicken resumed its pecking. "Don't forget you're a poet, not a chicken. Best to get back with the others. Right?"

The chicken looked up and said, "Yes, of course. And even though we have become chickens we are still working at our trade. How do you like this one?"

"We are glad that ants lack pants.
If they had them it would be confusing.
If an ant got into another ant's pants
The battle could be bruising."

"Oh noooo," they all said in chorus. "Get out of here!" They all charged the chicken who took to wing. It circled once, clucking loudly from above. As he began to climb back into the sky, they heard him say,

"For the ant in whose pants the other ant danced
Would be itching, as they say,
To swat the ant who danced in his pants
To make the itch go away."

Crystal started laughing and was soon joined by the lizard and the dragonfly. Aleister rolled his eyes again and said, "Listen, man. I was never into poetry except for Lobianko's limericks back in Lancaster. Let's move on and get through this."

"Aleister," Crystal began, "I think I'm going to fly over with the chickens. I don't like getting mud in my feathers."

"That's okay with me," Aleister answered, walking on. "If I could fly over with you, I'd do that."

"Leonard," Crystal addressed the palmetto bug. "I saw you crawl under Aleister's collar when the chicken started pecking at ants. It's safe to come now. He's gone."

"Thanks," Leonard answered as he stuck his first antenna out from his hiding place.

"If you would like to join me, you can ride on my back as I fly over this fracas ahead of us."

"That sounds good to me," answered the bug as he took to wing and landed on the goose's back. "If I get hit with a handful of mud, I could get squished."

"I think I'll join you," the dragonfly interjected. "I don't mind mud as long as it stays on the ground, but I could get hit with it too. You don't mind do you Aleister? And what about you two, Allen and Angelica?"

"Go ahead," they told her.

Aleister added, "We'll see you on the other side."

"I like mud," they could hear Jonathon the peach pit saying from Aleister's pocket.

As Crystal, Lee Ann and Leonard took off together, the others paused to watch them disappearing into the cloudless eastern sky.

The four approached the screaming masses. A double yellow line now marked their passage down the center of the road. Only Aleister managed to stay right on top of the centerline. The lizard's tail swished from side to side as he walked and his legs were too far apart to walk on the line, so his left feet stayed on the left side of the line and his right feet on the other. The spider stood taller than the other two and wider as well. So Angelica's feet landed with each step in the center of the opposing lanes. Only her body stayed centered above the double yellow line.

As the group approached the screaming crowds, some of their words became audible. "Tax and spend!" one group was yelling as clumps of mud sailed over the road.

"You grow rich exploiting the poor!" the other side yelled as the mud flew back.

"Open the borders! Let the poor flood in!" came another shout accompanied by a rain of mud.

"Close the borders!" came the reply. "You just want to exploit votes from people who can't speak English!"

Mud filled the air. Aleister had it in his hair and all over his face. His clothing was splattered. His feet sloshed with each step, mud oozing from his shoes. Just under the sound of the raging din, Aleister could hear the voice of Jonathon Peach. "This is wonderful. I haven't felt this good since you guys dropped in and dug me up. "

Glancing over his shoulder with concern for his other two companions, Aleister could see they too were covered with mud. Angelica kept busy brushing it away from the air vents she used for breathing, located on both sides of her body. There was so much mud that Aleister was having a problem staying on the double yellow line in the middle of the road. The lizard was having no problems. As the mud hit him, he just swished his tail and the mud flew back in the direction it came from, but this was causing some problems.

Suddenly, Aleister heard a voice from the left raised above the others in anger. "Why are you middle-of-the-roaders throwing mud at us and not at them?"

Other voices joined the first and soon mud was coming heavily from the left aimed directly at Aleister's party. They hurried on, but Aleister realized Angelica was growing angry. The lizard swished his tail again and this time the mud flew to the right.

Now a voice came from the right with the same demanding question. "Hey! Lizard! Why you throwin' that mud at us? You fake middle-of-the-roaders are pretendin' just to get closer so you can get us with the mud better!"

With that, the intensity of the mud bombardment at least tripled. Some of it missed them and went over the road to the left hitting others over there. This infuriated the left-siders and they too increased the bombardment so now the party of four was getting directly lambasted heavily from both sides. Aleister was growing angry too.

Suddenly, he stopped. The lizard and the spider stopped. Aleister wiped a handful of mud off of his face, furiously slammed it to the pavement and shouted at the top of lungs, "STOP! You people are nothing but a bunch of mud wallowing swine! If you could drop your jargon and actually talk to each other, you might get something done instead of just getting dirtier."

To Aleister's utter shock, all the people within earshot on both sides of the road turned into mud wallowing swine. They were happily rolling in the mud, frolicking and chasing each other. The bombardment stopped.

"Well." Aleister found himself almost too surprised to speak. "What do you think of that?"

A voice coming from Aleister's pocket mournfully cried out, "Aleister! What have you done? Where has all the mud gone? Bring me more mud!"

With the end of the flying mud, the group trudged on till they arrived at the tower. They found it to be just as they chickens described it. One door bore a sign saying "Entrance" and no exit could be seen. The tower reached so high in the sky, Aleister could barely see the top of it. Around the base of the tower, people could be seen from time to time dressed in black robes, heads covered in black hoods. On the backs of their robes, words were stenciled, "Secret Servants."

They carried boxes or trays of food to the entrance. There, they handed what they were carrying to others inside the entrance. Aleister saw a line of them on the other side of the tower with boxes heaped with money. These boxes were placed on a conveyor belt that entered the tower through a window three stories up.

The tower stood in the center of a huge round-about. At the entrance to the round-about, signs warned the weary traveler to not get too close to the building because of "Flying Garbage."

Aleister was still trying to get the mud off his arms and hands as he walked, so he didn't notice the signs at first. Suddenly, a half a ton of trash smashed into the ground, right in front of Aleister. He leaped back. "Gee! That could have hit me!"

"Check the sign," advised the lizard. "This garbage comes from the very top. I saw that one coming."

Aleister did just that. At the bottom of the sign warning about the garbage, some graffiti artist had scrawled, "Money in. Garbage out."

Just then, a front-end-loader and a small dump truck came hurrying up to collect the new affluence from the very top of the ivory tower.

Chapter 14: Letharland

After they passed the tower, everything grew quiet. The arguers and mudslingers had broken for lunch and withdrawn from the road to pavilions and small diners that appeared in the distance. The drying mud on Aleister's clothing flaked from him as he walked. The spider picked it off herself as she strolled along behind the lizard. Soon the road began climbing. The incline of the road increased so gently that Aleister didn't notice it at first. As it grew steeper, he eventually realized he was getting winded from climbing. He stopped, raising his eyes to look ahead. Another forest appeared in the distance. Beyond the top of the rise he could see white birds perched in some of the trees. As they drew nearer, Aleister saw many people sitting in the shade, some reclining in the grass, others pacing.

As they approached the grove, a goose came waddling out of the shade to greet them. "Welcome to Letharland," she groaned through a yawn. "Everything's so relaxed here. Do I know you?"

"Crystal!" Aleister exclaimed emphatically, hurrying toward her. "Of course you know us."

His words were cut short by the flapping of wings as three chickens descended from one of the nearby trees.

"Is my name Crystal? I sort of remember that." The goose's thoughts were evidently wandering.

"Bartemus," Aleister greeted one of the chickens. "What's going on here? Why doesn't Crystal know us?"

"This is Letharland," explained the chicken. "The name is a corruption of the word 'Lethargy.' Once one falls into this place, it's very hard to continue any journey." The chicken plucked for a moment at one of its feathers then continued. "In those trees flow the headwaters of the River Lethe [leethee]. Anyone who drinks its water forgets their past and history. Fortunately, this far upstream, it hasn't gathered all of its power, so people here in Letharland who drink from it can be reminded who they are; or, as one might put it, 'who they were.' Letharland changes everyone who drinks from the River Lethe."

"How did you find this out?" Aleister wondered.

"By watching."

The palmetto bug, still riding on the goose's back ,called out, "I could have stopped her, but I didn't know yet. I watched it happen to Crystal. Oh why didn't I stop her?"

The dragonfly came zooming out of the trees and landed on Aleister's shoulder. "Don't drink the water here," she advised him.

"Angelica, Leonard," Aleister called to his friends. "You heard all this, right? We can't drink the water from the stream."

"Look out!" yelled the lizard. "Get off the road!"

They all leaped off the road just in time to miss being struck by a huge, round boulder, rolling at high speed down the hill. In the distance, behind the boulder, they saw a husky man wearing only cut-off shorts, chasing the boulder. "What's that all about?" Aleister demanded of no one in particular.

"That man comes by here about twice every day," a young woman in a brown sweat shirt, jeans and sandals volunteered. She approached them from the shade of the trees and, yawning, continued. "He says his name is Syphus or something like that and he has to push that rock over the top of the hill, but every time he gets near the top, he slips and the rock gets away from him. It must be muddy up there."

Aleister took a seat in the grass. Crystal came closer and he began stroking her feathers. Thoughtfully, he reflected half to himself, "But this is Never Ever Land. It's not Hades — is it?"

"What's the difference?" retorted the lizard. "The River Lethe is right over there. Sisyphus is here with his boulder."

"I don't want to learn about anything else that's in Never Ever Land," muttered Aleister getting to his feet. "You're talking about fiction becoming reality. It's not fiction that lethargy is crippling to anyone willing to submit to it. I'm not staying here for a single minute. Let's get out of here!" With that, Aleister went back to the road and started to climb.

"I have a feeling that I should stay with you," Crystal muttered as she waddled after him.

The man who chased the boulder now rested a short distance from them. The lizard called out to him, "Hey Syphus. Join us! We're leaving Never Ever Land to slay the Evil Queen and put an end to this place."

Syphus stood. He looked down the hill where his boulder had gone. Then he looked back at the departing group. "I can't leave," he protested. "I have too much time invested in this. I'm sure I can succeed, if I just keep trying."

"Doing the same thing over and over and expecting different results is insane," Aleister called over his shoulder. "Think about it. Give it up. Join us. Help us do something productive and positive!"

"I'll think about it," Syphus called back to him, scratching his head.

Aleister stopped and turned to face the grove of trees they called Letharland. "What about the rest of you? Are you going to lay around in Letharland till you die or are you going to take charge of your lives? Join us! We're leaving this place." He waited. You're all writers aren't you? Do you believe in yourselves? Do you believe in your work?"

Thirty or more had risen to their feet. He could see their brows furrowing in determination as they approached the road. "We've spent a lot of time here," one of them called out. "How can we leave all this?"

"Leave all what?" shouted Aleister. "What are you accomplishing here? What have done here? What have you written here? Shake off your self-doubts and join us. What have you got to lose, another sip from the Lethe?" With that, Aleister turned and began marching up the hill, lips tight, brows crossed and angry determination radiating from every pore.

"You should have been a preacher," the palmetto bug snickered.

"Look," urged the dragonfly. "They're coming. And look, the chickens are on the wing. I guess their flock mentality saved the ones who drank from the stream."

Aleister glanced over his shoulder and saw that a crowd of around fifty people now followed them. Some carried bags of food. Others slung bedrolls over their shoulders. All were dressed in rags and all of them looked hungry and angry. A large cloud of chickens ascended from the trees and flew on before them. Looking farther back, he noticed with some satisfaction that Syphus was catching up to him.

"So," he chided with a touch of pomp in his voice. "Doing the same thing over and over and expecting different results is insane, is it?"

"Yes," affirmed Aleister defiantly.

"How many times and to how many agents and publishing houses have you submitted only to be rudely and abruptly rejected?" asked Syphus innocently.

"Hundreds!" responded Aleister, fully aware of where Syphus was going with this. "Why?" Aleister stopped and glared up at Syphus. Aleister was at least a foot shorter and a hundred pounds lighter but he felt full of fight.

"Just wondered," Syphus murmured. "Why would you expect different results if you try it again?"

Aleister continued his climb up the long hill. "Just before I started that stupid job with Flaass, I found a wonderful editor who was helping me understand why I was getting rejected. I believe with her help, I can become successful."

"Sounds like a pipe dream to me," offered Syphus. "But I guess it holds more hope than pushing a rock up a hill and chasing it down again over and over."

"Whether it does or not, I am committed to the project," Aleister stated simply. With his tone growing fierce, he added. "And I will succeed or die trying. The first thing I have to do is leave Never Ever Land."

"I think I'd rather roll the rock over and over. At least I know it's hopeless. What you're doing gives you false hope. That's heartbreaking."

"Get away from me," Aleister snapped.

"What's that up ahead," called out the palmetto bug. Leonard had been listening to the conversation but never took his eyes off the horizon.

"It's the top of the hill," answered Syphus. "I've never been beyond it, but from here it looks like the end of the world. It just sort of seems to drop off. Look there," he pointed at tracks on the ground. "That's where I always slipped, losing the rock."

"It does seem a bit muddy," observed the dragonfly. "I can see why he always slips here."

Just as she said that, Syphus slipped and landed right on his bottom in the mud. He got up laughing and remarked, "Well. That was different."

"How's that?" asked Aleister still a little annoyed.

"I didn't lose the rock." His expression stiffened with determination. He took a deep breath and said, "Maybe now it's me who has false hope, but at least I know I can go back to my rock. Let's keep going."

At the very top of the hill stood a small sign written on a flat board, mounted on a single post. It said "Borderlands."

Bartemus chose that moment to make his appearance by landing on the sign. The crowd stopped in surprise. The last thing the new additions to the entourage expected was to see a chicken coming out of the sky. "Ahem," Bartemus uttered loudly enough to get their attention. The crowd quieted. "There's a snake path of sorts over there to the right. It winds its way down the hill, but it's only narrow for a short distance. Then it widens into the valley below."

"Who's the chicken?" someone called out.

"What's he saying?" someone toward the rear wanted to know.

"At the bottom of the mountain lies a river and I think it's part of the Lethe. Don't drink from it." The chicken spotted a bug on the ground and hopped off the sign to peck it up. Then he continued. "About half a mile beyond the river stands a huge brick wall. It must be twenty feet high and there are no doors or gates. None of us had the courage to fly over it."

"Why not?" demanded Aleister. "We have to find out what's on the other side. That has to be where the Evil Queen lives."

"We decided to wait for the rest of you," the chicken called over its wing as it took off and dived into the valley, "before we go over to the other side, just in case it really is 'the dark side.' "

The dismal climb down the steep part of the path could have been less gloomy without the grumbling from the frustrated people from Letharland. Leaving their safe but hopeless existence, the safety of their surroundings and The Lethe, their stream of forgetfulness, seemed now to be a dangerous and pointless choice. Being away from that place, many of them were beginning to remember who they were, including Crystal Gooseworthy. So the discontent with the loss of their safety was being replaced with anger at the lost time and hopeless existence they had there. Their catharsis was incredible.

"I can't believe I did that," Crystal remonstrated many times as she half waddled and half glided down the steep, winding path. "That water was like a drug. One minute I was me and the next I was a silly goose."

Many of the people joining them were much angrier about having been trapped in that place. "It seems that some of them may have been there for years," the lizard remarked after listening to a number of them. Their disillusionment ranged from simple complaining to full fledged rage.

"We choose what we choose," Aleister snapped half in anger. "I have no sympathy for them. Life is about choices." He wiped some sweat from his face, slipped on a loose rock and nearly lost his footing. "The end, or whatever this path holds for us, is getting close. The chicken reported seeing a tall brick wall. If we can't knock it down maybe we can find some ropes with grappling hooks or something like that."

"It sounds like the land of the Evil Queen is well protected," the palmetto bug muttered. "Angelica the spider and I can probably just walk up the wall. Crystal and Lee Ann the dragonfly can just buzz right over the top with the chickens but I don't know how the rest of you are going to make it."

"We'll find a way," Aleister assured him with a touch of impatience.

"We didn't come this far to be stopped by something as simple as a pile of bricks."

"There's something I've been meaning to ask you," the lizard began.

"What's that?" came Aleister's response.

"How did you change all those mudslingers back there into hogs? That was something to behold. One moment they were political fundamentalists and the next they were hogs in their wallow. How did you do that? Are you a secret literary agent?"

"They didn't change into anything," Aleister explained, as much to himself as to Allen. "They just believed me. I was right, you know."

"Whatever you did was like what Flaass and Beth did to us. They announced a thing and suddenly it was true," the lizard persisted. "I haven't seen anyone else do anything like that."

"This is Never Ever Land. I even saw a man floating up a stream, three feet above the water. He was standing in a bucket, holding himself up by the handle."

"Wow," chuckled the lizard. "Where was that?"

"Behind Coulter's Lounge. You were dozing on the lawn."

"I don't mean to interrupt," the palmetto bug cut in. "But look down there below us. Are those flying monkeys or not?"

Chapter 15: The Evil Queen

Aleister's entourage neared the bottom of the mountain. Thick forest surrounded them. Their numbers had grown to more than he could count, stretching out of sight behind him on the trail. Foliage filled every space under the trees. Aleister thought he saw vervain, hyssop, wild cucumber and every manner of fern. The chickens were roosting peacefully in the trees among winged monkeys and squirrels.

"The monkeys make me feel a little nervous," Crystal the goose grumbled, looking around apprehensively. Her memories had been coming back quickly since they crested the hill, now far behind them. "They aren't that sickly green color we saw before in Bethland and Flaassland."

"That's a relief." Aleister's neck was getting stiff from watching the monkeys high everhead. "But their blue color isn't very comforting. I wonder who these belong to."

"All you had to do was ask," a voice overhead answered him.

Standing close behind, Syphus bent over quickly and picked up a fallen branch he could use for a club. Aleister froze in his tracks. His growing nervousness over being in the Borderlands had him jumpy about what kind of resistance they would meet. Crystal looked up, squawked once and began backing away. The spider lifted its two front legs preparing to strike. The lizard glanced quickly around looking for a hole to dive into but settled on a pile of fallen leaves. It started edging in that direction.

Aleister slowly raised his eyes. Perched on the tree limb just over his head sat a blue, winged monkey. Right next to the monkey, the mockingbird they met in Flaassland screeched in the monkey's ear, "They're the ones I told you about! They're coming to kill the Queen! They're dangerous! Look how their numbers have grown! They have to be stopped!"

Growing weary of the noise, the monkey swatted at the bird who flew to a higher branch out of reach. From there it started that dreadful hissing noise that mockingbirds make when they see cats near their nests.

"So. Who are the blue monkeys?" Aleister asked.

The monkey shifted its weight on the tree and, wrapping its tail around the limb supporting it, replied guardedly, "we serve the Queen you have come to kill, if the mockingbird tells it truly. And who, may I ask, are you?"

Aleister rubbed the back of his neck, looked down at his feet briefly then back at the monkey. "We are writers, all of us. We have been used and abused and now have been trapped in Never Ever Land."

"We're here to find the Evil Queen and end Never Ever Land," shouted Leonard the palmetto bug on Aleister's shoulder. Just *look* at what's been done to us! We demand retribution!"

The lizard had completely concealed itself under the leaves. Angelica the spider lowered her two front legs, listening quietly. The monkey laughed and said, "If you can find the border, and if you can get across it, you might find her. If you do, I think you will not find what you expected." The monkey unwrapped its tail from around the tree limb, stood and stretched its wings to take off. It smiled and said, "She knows you're coming, of course," and flew away.

"We must be getting pretty close," Aleister whispered to those nearest. Looking around at those behind them, he added, "It might be a good idea for us to all pick up something we can use to fight with. Those monkeys will most likely try to defend her."

"I can peck pretty hard," Crystal announced grimly.

"And I still have my sting," Angelica the spider grimly announced.

"Let's move on, then," Aleister suggested half to himself as he continued down the path through the forest.

Fluttering overhead drew their eyes aloft again. The blue, winged monkeys were all lifting off and heading east. In just moments, all them had disappeared, leaving only the squirrels and birds.

"Where are they going?" Crystal watched them disappearing.

"Who cares?" retorted the palmetto bug. "I'm glad they're gone."

Around a bend in the path, the river appeared. Its narrowness deceptively concealed its power. The current was strong and the smooth surface concealed its depth. "Bartemus mentioned this," Aleister reminded them. "Don't drink its water."

The path turned to the left, following the flow of the stream. The party continued along its way and as they rounded a large outcropping of rocks, they found a narrow footbridge. Beyond the bridge stood the brick wall.

As they crossed the bridge, each member of the party walked up to the wall, one at a time, felt it and took a seat on the ground. The chicken/poets were resting in the trees above. Bartemus, the chicken-union leader, landed at Aleister's feet. It looked up at him expectantly and with a soft cluck, it asked, "Now what, chief?"

Aleister rose to his feet and looked up toward the top of the wall. As far as he could see in both directions, the top of the wall was lined with winged, blue monkeys. The grumbling around him grew louder as he wracked his brains about how to get over the wall. "Hey, monkeys," he yelled at the top of voice. "How do we get over the wall?"

One of the monkeys spread its wings and jumped from the wall. Gliding to a stop on the ground in front of Aleister, it asked, "Please excuse my ignorance but what wall would that be?"

"The wall you just jumped off of, naturally. What do you mean 'what wall?' "

"But there is no wall," announced the monkey quite reasonably. "It's an impenetrable forest with tall trees and dense undergrowth. No one can pass through there. It's too dangerous and dense. There are large carnivorous animals. No one goes in there."

Suddenly, the wall vanished. To Aleister's stunned amazement he saw a thick forest and heard the calls of large animals, the crackling of underbrush as they ran toward him. He trembled in fear and was about to turn and run when the monkey said, "Oh. Wait a minute. I was mistaken. I'm so sorry. It's not a forest but a huge mountain with straight up and down cliffs, far too steep for anyone to climb. But there's a tunnel right over there." It pointed to Aleister's left. "If you look into it, you might see a light at the other end, but it's quite far. You might not be able to see the other end from here, at all."

Aleister gasped as the forest vanished and a mountain appeared in its place. All of Aleister's entourage gradually backed away toward the stream, eyes wide in fear and confusion. Aleister glanced to the left where the monkey said they could find a tunnel. Just as it had said, a large opening appeared in the side of the mountain. Aleister began moving toward it when the monkey stopped him. "Was I mistaken again?" wondered the monkey in mock confusion. "It's not a mountain but a seashore. You're facing the ocean. The waves are crashing loudly. Seagulls are squawking..."

"Just stop right now!" Crystal demanded. "Enough is enough!"

Aleister turned to her in surprise, and was he ever surprised. Crystal, no longer a goose, stood there in her faded jeans, torn sweatshirt, eyes flashing in rage and shouting at a blue monkey. He turned back to the monkey and was startled to find a hauntingly beautiful young woman in a flowing white dress. Her nearly black hair reached her shoulders and she wore a wide smile on her face. She waited patiently, while recognition settled into Aleister's mind. It was H'eung Yau, the super-model of his dream.

In his startled condition he almost ignored the struggling in his pants pocket. He frantically reached in and pulled out the peach pit, rapidly becoming a short plump red headed man with a day's growth of beard on his cheeks and chin.

Leonard DeMolier was standing just behind him, wide eyed, trying to figure out what happened to the brick wall. "Uh, what's going on?" he ventured.

"Writers have wonderful imaginations," the young woman began. "But you have to draw a line somewhere, between where your imagination ends and reality begins." She looked around the gathering crowd that had been following Aleister from Never Ever Land. "And above all, you must *NEVER EVER* allow someone else to control your imagination! If someone tells you that you are a goose," she turned her gaze to Crystal, "*don't BELIEVE them*! That someone says a thing doesn't make it true, no matter how much you respect his opinion. That person is still just a human being and it is still just an opinion."

"Are you the evil queen?" asked Aleister innocently.

The young woman started laughing. "A friend of mine, John Lennon, once said, 'Reality leaves a lot to the imagination.' You can call me Joanna." She half turned as though to leave. "All of reality is the Land of Imagination and you have been living on the dark side. There is no such darkness on this side." She took a deep breath and sighed before continuing.

"To them, I am the evil queen. They hate me there because I made it on my own with no literary agent. My name is Joanna. Would any of you like some tea? Come."

Behind them stood the forest. Just within its trees, a stream gurgled past. Before them grew a manicured lawn lined and filled with small flower gardens. A cottage nestled among the patches of flowers, a few hundred feet away.

"I'm sorry for the way I teased you," Joanna apologized simply. "I had to shock you out of the trance you formed to convince yourself of how dark life is and how accurate Ronald Flaass's assessment of your abilities might be."

They reached the rear door of the cottage and Joanna held the door while everybody filed in. Aleister was amazed that the small cottage was big enough inside to accommodate everyone.

"Just because your poetry or books received a few rejections," Joanna continued, "doesn't mean your life is over and it doesn't mean your work is no good. The problem could be as simple as the phase of the moon."

"How do we get home from here?" Angelica the former spider politely inquired.

"Oh. I have a mirror," Joanna smiled. "But before you go back through the mirror, I want to give you a list of editor's names who can help you polish your books. That may improve your chances for publication."

"When we go through the mirror," Crystal began, "where will we be?"

"Central Park, of course," Joanna answered as though it was the most natural thing possible. "What book do you intend to start with next, Aleister?"

Aleister grinned broadly. "I have three, right here on my thumb disc, but I'm going to start a new one as soon as I get home. I'm going to call it *Aleister Through the Looking Glass*," but I'm going to use a pseudonym."

"What name are you going to use?" Crystal chuckled, swiping her hair out of her eyes.

"My pseudonym is Robert G. Makin" he replied proudly. "Do you like it?"

"The name itself is a bit bland," Joanna remarked off handedly. "Why don't you come up with something a little jazzier, like Louis L'Amore or something like that?"

"I think it's already been used. Besides, I don't want my work to sell because of a jazzy author's name. I want it to sell because it's worth buying and reading."

"A worthy intention," Joanna applauded.

"I've written a poem for all this," announced Jonathon the former peach pit peach. "I wrote this for authors everywhere, who had to spend time in Never Ever Land getting jerked around by uncaring agents and publishers. I am calling it, *An Eschatological Daydream*. Wanna hear it?"

"Yeah, go for it," came the reply. As Joanna poured everyone another cup of tea and passed around cookies, Jonathon began.

An Eschatological Daydream
by Jonathon Peach (Pitt):

The sun shall rise again tomorrow,
For it's been gone so very long,
That all the rain and clouds of sorrow
Began to think the sunlight wrong.
Then all the birds shall sing its glory,
Rainbows shine ten thousand strong.
All of those who rise to see it
Will swear of how the Sun Belongs.

About the Author

Robert G. Makin found his life paths growing up on Laurel Mountain. There he became friends with Elves and Flying Squirrels, did spelunking at Wild Cat Rocks and listened at the feet of his grandfathers to the stories of the Railroad, the Steel Mills and the Old Country. Bits and pieces of Old German and ancient Scottish Gaelic still creep into his conversation from those days gone by. A degree in Fanciful Literature from Indiana University of Pennsylvania fueled his drive to learn more about Elven History and their social structure. He sought fulfillment at Lancaster Theological Seminary of the United Church of Christ where he discovered Essenism, some of the precursors of Biblical History and the stories told to Abraham as Abraham sat at the feet of his grandfathers. They were stories of Nanna, Ningur, Inanna, Ya and Enlil, at the birth of Human Kind. Makin found that there is no history quite like oral history, nor quite as honest. Some truths have been politically incorrect for millennia and forbidden from written histories. Some truths have been corrected and updated to fit what's popular. Makin has found them hidden in Social Artifacts and takes pleasure in their unraveling and revelation.

Makin earned his bread for many years by selling opinions. Today he spends his time, sharing his love for and the history of St. Augustine, Florida with visitors from all over the world who come to hear his tales. In StrathNaver Legends, Makin expresses the exuberant mysticism of the unknown, the what-if's, the maybe's and the things that very well may have been, like friendships with Flying Squirrels and Elves.

Other Books by
Robert G. Makin
Available at Amazon, Barnes & Noble and other book sellers

Strathnaver Legends

The heart of a quiet, peaceful village, ripped open by the remorseless vitriol of a sadistic predator, drives kith and kin on a hunt for the hunter. Falling in with unknown races and cultures, they are forced to overcome prejudice and distrust in their drive for a common interest, to live in freedom from terror.

The Faces of Inanna

An ancient evil plaguing a small area of the South Pacific has been the focus of an equally ancient, very secret fraternity for hundreds of years. Why were the neighboring islanders driven to insane wars, the deforestation of their islands and illogical religions demanding human sacrifices? "The Watchers" had to resolve the conflict, but could they? Finally, the Ascended Brotherhood designated one man to stand as a fence between the good and the evil. Imagine his surprise upon learning the enigma they so long withstood was a very special woman.

Return to Masada

The historic Battle of Masada has become a symbol of freedom, hope and courage to die, if necessary, for one's principles. Makin delivers a new version of this famous "David and Goliath" struggle of the Jewish people against the Roman Army.

www.ingramcontent.com/pod-product-compliance
Lightning Source LLC
Chambersburg PA
CBHW070912030726
47504CB00005B/1561